Gideon Dickinson

Poems and Essays

Including the fallen chief, the Minstrel's Curse, Kenilworth ...

Gideon Dickinson

Poems and Essays
Including the fallen chief, the Minstrel's Curse, Kenilworth ...

ISBN/EAN: 9783744708159

Printed in Europe, USA, Canada, Australia, Japan

Cover: Foto ©Andreas Hilbeck / pixelio.de

More available books at **www.hansebooks.com**

POEMS AND ESSAYS:

INCLUDING

THE FALLEN CHIEF, THE MINSTREL'S CURSE,
KENILWORTH, TRIBUTES TO HOLMES AND
LONGFELLOW, BOOTH AS HAMLET,
THE WIZARD'S GRAVE.

ALSO

EARLY AND JUVENILE POEMS, AND TRANSLATIONS
FROM THE GERMAN;

WITH SOME ACCOUNT OF

Minstrels and Minstrelsy of the Middle Ages,

AND

EARLY BALLAD-POETRY OF DIFFERENT
NATIONS.

BY

GIDEON DICKINSON.

"It is the voice of years that are gone;
They roll before me with all their deeds."

"Sic bolvere Parcas."

BOSTON:

A. WILLIAMS AND COMPANY,

Old Corner Bookstore.

1883.

PRESS OF RAND, AVERY, AND COMPANY,
BOSTON.

PREFACE.

THE following poems are a part of many which have been composed by the author, during his hours of leisure, while practicing an uncongenial and perplexing profession. Some of them were called forth by passing events of the times; while others are the mere offspring of his own fancy in hours of meditation. The longer ones are, with few exceptions, of comparatively recent composition; but to them are added a few which were composed in the early years of the author's life, —from his sixteenth year upward, —and which may therefore be termed "early" and "juvenile" poems. In selecting from his manuscripts those which were to be given to the public in this little volume, the author was not always moved by the belief that the ones selected were better, or possessed more merit, than others which might be given in their places. But, merely, he chooses to publish these at the present time, and to withhold others, which may perhaps possess more literary merit, from the fact that they contain allusions to persons yet living, which it would be

more proper to make public after they cease to be actors
on the world's stage. The author is by no means blind
to the imperfections of these trifles, and especially is he
aware of the defects of the ones composed in early youth;
and he could easily give to them now a better dress and
more finished appearance : but that is what he least
wishes to do; for then they would cease to be the familiar children and companions of his early years.[1] In their
present form they bring back ever to his mind the memory of other days and years now passed and gone for
ever, repeopling them with dear delightful friends, now
changed or far away, or—sadder still—too often repeopling them with dear, dear friends now dead and
gone for ever. Therefore he chooses to see such early
poems in the old familiar dress they always wore; for, to
him, —

"A stone unturned
Is sweeter than a strange or altered face;
A tree that flings its shadow as of yore
Will make the blood stir, sometimes, when the words
Of a long-looked-for lip fall icy cold."

---

[1] In regard to the poems written in boyhood and early youth, I could
say with Wordsworth on a similar occasion, that "it would be easy
to amend them now both as to sentiment and expression;" but, in the
case of early and juvenile poems, such emendations are always made
"at the risk of injuring those characteristic features which, after all,
will be regarded as the principal recommendation of all juvenile poems."

If it shall be asked, " Why publish them at all?" the author will answer, that, being inclined to studious habits and somewhat given to meditation, he could not always resist the temptation of putting his thoughts into written form; and, such being the case, they have accumulated to such an extent that it has now become necessary to make some disposition of them; and so, with the distinguished author of " A Fable for Critics," he will say, that —

" These trifles, composed to please only himself
  And his own private fancy, were laid on the shelf,
  Till some friends, who had seen them, induced him, by dint
  Of saying they liked them, to put them in print;
  That is, having come to that very conclusion,
  He consulted them when it could make no confusion."

And, if these trifles shall meet with the same kind consideration which has been accorded to some already given to the public, the author will soon publish another volume, containing a series of poems upon Scottish subjects, — poems descriptive of Scottish scenes, personages, and events, — which were composed during a journey through some of the most picturesque portions of that land of chivalry, romance, and song, where the pilgrim ever walks upon enchanted ground, — a land made deeply interesting by deeds of historic fame, and filled with decaying ruins of moldering palaces and crumbling towers, time-worn cathedrals, and castles in decay.

G. D.

December, 1882.

CONTENTS.

CONTENTS.

L'ENVOI.

Child of my brain and offspring of the heart,
 The fleeting hours have rolled o'er thee and me,
 Till now the hour has come when we must part ;
 And thou alone shalt dare the world's dark sea,
 While I must vainly wait and watch for thee,
 Fearing lest evil tidings from thee come :
 For well I know the dangers of that sea
  Where thou, unaided, art compelled to roam,
Seeking, perchance in vain, for sympathy and home.

But go thou forth into the heartless world,
 And meet its scorn and hatred with a smile ;
 For scorn and hatred at thee shall be hurled,
 Yet bear thee bravely on thy course the while ;
 And, if with flattering speech some should beguile,
 Prove well their fair words ere thou deem'st them true ;
 For hatred often lurks beneath a smile,
  And poisoned fruits are fairest to the view :
But, trusting thee to Fate, I bid thee now adieu.

POEMS AND ESSAYS.

BIOGRAPHICAL INTRODUCTION TO THE FALLEN CHIEF.

JAMES ABRAM GARFIELD was the twentieth President of the United States.[1] He was born in the little town of Orange, Ohio, on the 19th of November, 1831. He suffered, in his youth, all the privations and hardships of Western pioneer life. Left an orphan in earliest life, he succeeded, by his own efforts, in obtaining a collegiate education; and became, afterwards, first a teacher of Latin and Greek, and then a college president. He also studied law, and was admitted to the bar. When the civil war broke out, he entered the Union army as colonel of the 42d Ohio Volunteers, and was ordered to the front in December, 1861. In the army he was distinguished as a brave and very competent officer. His military record was a brilliant one. He took part in the great battles of Shiloh and Chickamauga, and was made

---

[1] He was the seventeenth President, counting only those persons who were regularly chosen to the office of President; but three former Vice-Presidents became Presidents by reason of the death of the Presidents of their times.

a major-general of volunteers "for gallant and meritorious services" in the last-named battle.

He afterwards served several years in the Congress of the United States as a member from the State of Ohio. And, at the Republican National Convention which met at Chicago in June, 1880, General Garfield was chosen, after the convention had been sitting for ten days, as the candidate of the party for the presidency. At the national election, November, 1880, he was elected by a handsome majority to the presidency of the United States. In the spring of 1881 he left his happy home in Mentor, Ohio, to go on to Washington and assume the duties of President, and took the oath of office and was inaugurated on Friday, the 4th of March, 1881, with ceremonies of unusual magnificence. But, alas! that happy home in dear old Mentor, where he had passed some of the happiest years of his life, surrounded by his mother, wife, and loving children,—that happy home which he had so recently left with regret and a heavy heart,—that happy home he was doomed never again to revisit in life; for, on the 2d of July following, while passing through the railroad depot in Washington, to take the cars with the intention of making a trip northward for rest and recreation, he was shot down from behind, and mortally wounded, by a miserable assassin, —one Guiteau,—a disappointed and crack-brained politician, who confessed to have been dogging him for weeks with the intention of killing him. The assassin was immediately arrested, and imprisoned to suffer the penalty of his crime. The wounded President was carefully taken up, and tenderly cared for; and from that fatal 2d of July, until the nineteenth day of September, he lingered on through eighty long and heart-rending days of suffering, pain, and sorrow, where faint rays of hope often alternated with shadows of despair, till exhausted nature at length gave out; and, surrounded by his anxious, weeping wife and children, he calmly breathed his last, and was at rest; and a united nation, bowed down in sorrow, mourned his loss with quivering lips and floods of burning tears.

THE FALLEN CHIEF.

"After life's fitful fever, he sleeps well;
   Treason has done his worst: nor steel, nor poison
   Malice domestic, foreign levy, nothing,
   Can touch him further!"

                              Macbeth, Act iii. Scene 2.

O GOD, behold a prostrate State![1]
   O Christ, incline thy gracious ear!
O God, avert such dreadful fate!
   O Christ, in mercy, wilt thou hear?
O God, a nation bends the knee!
   O Christ, behold a nation's grief!
O God, a nation prays to thee!
   O Father! Saviour! spare our Chief!

Such, such the prayer, the suppliant cry,
   Which a united nation gave:
Their mingled voices, through the sky,
   Prayed God their honored Chief to save.

---

[1] While President Garfield was slowly but surely sinking from the effects of his mortal wound, a day of public fasting and prayer was appointed to be held, in which both churches and people heartily joined in prayers to God for his recovery. All places of business were closed; all labor suspended for the day, which was universally and solemnly observed.

14

A nation's women poured their tears —
   Their burning tears — in sight of Heaven,
And sighed their tender, soul-felt prayers,
   That life to him might yet be given.

But not a nation's burning tears
   Could change the fixed decrees of Heaven,
And to a nation's mingled prayers
   No answer from on high was given.
Weak man, rejoice! God's ways are sure:
   Effect shall ever follow cause;
Millions of worlds all rest secure
   Through his unchanged, unchanging laws.

Then why repine at what he sends?
   Why pray to change his fixed decree?
Whate'er is best for noble ends,
   God, and God only, can foresee!
'Tis true, our noble, honored Chief
   By an assassin's hand lies low;
'Tis true, our hearts are bowed with grief:
   But God — for good — decreed it so.

He died with honor, and his bed
Is with the noble, sainted dead,
And the world's history shall enshrine
His noble deeds and death sublime.
He died — but wrote his shining name
The highest on the scroll of fame,

And ever there his name shall shine
A beacon-light through coming time.

A hundred bards have sung his fame, —
Bards of renown and noble name ;
The gray-haired bards, before whose eyes
The visioned future open lies ;
And infant bards, whose souls of fire
Are toying with the unproved lyre.
They all have brought — both young and old —
Their harp's rich treasures, — songs of gold ;
And shall I — humblest of the throng —
Forget to weave a requiem song ?

Shall I sit sorrowing in gloom,
Nor weave one garland for his tomb ?
No ! let my harp her slumbers break,
And let poetic thought awake !
Let my hand wake each tuneful string
While I my humble tribute bring, —
A tribute for our noble Chief,
And her whose heart is bowed in grief, —
A chaplet for our Chief's dark tomb,
And her whose soul is wrapped in gloom.

The autumn winds, hoarse, loud, and strong,
Shall sing his solemn requiem song ;
The drifting snows, in winter gloom,
Shall spread their mantle o'er his tomb ;

But never shall his palsied ear
The solemn winds of autumn hear,
And never shall he wake to know
The chill of winter's drifted snow,
And never can he feel the sting
That Malice' poisoned words can bring.

" After life's fitful fever, he
Sleeps well" in calm tranquillity;
" Treason has done his worst," and now
No care can cloud his noble brow;
" Malice domestic" ne'er can come
To sting him in his happy home;
Nor " foreign levy," — on strange shore, —
" Nor steel, nor poison, touch him " more.
He sleeps in peace; and we must all
Deplore his sad, untimely fall.

But, bowed with grief, we say, with pride,
A hero lived! a martyr died!
For his loved country Garfield gave
His life, and filled a martyr's grave;
And Freedom's goddess, free from stain,
Now consecrates his noble name.
His body sleeps beneath the sod;
His soul, in peace, rests with his God.

For what he was and what he dared,
Remember him for aye;

And that his memory be spared,
　We evermore will pray.

Let a united country bend,
　And give him grateful tear;
Let party strife for ever end;
　Let concord re-appear!

No North, no South, no East, no West:
　He died alike for all!
United, they are strong and blest;
　Divided, they would fall.

Let politicians cease their strife,
　Their vulture-greed forego:
Their shameless quarrels cost his life, —
　His, and poor Lincoln's, too.

Oh, let all discord in the State
　For ever buried be!
Let love fraternal, free from hate,
　Our future motto be.

The world will blush for shame to see,
　And Freedom's sun go down,
If Freedom's price so oft must be
　A martyr's bloody crown!

Give we our pity now to those
Whose cup is filled with earthly woes:
His aged mother, bowed with years, —
What words can dry her burning tears?
She, who so fondly doted on
Her lost and murdered darling son, —
What words can paint the wretched woe
That her last, saddened years must know?
Weighed down with years, and bowed with grief,
E'en death to her would bring relief;
And she will pray full soon to meet
Her dear lost son at Jesus' feet.
She loved, as only mothers love:
With him she soon shall meet above.

But his poor widowed wife! what eye
Can view her grief, and still be dry?
Her bursting heart, ah! who can weigh
Its anguish when he passed away?
When, kneeling by his lifeless form,
To her caress came no return:
Then joy expired, and hope sank low,
And her sad soul was wrapped in woe;
And, ever now, in darkened gloom
She dwells, as in a living tomb.
To her, oh! how can minstrel sing?
To her, what comfort can he bring?
I strike the chords of hope, and, lo!
My wailing harp gives notes of woe!

Her sole remaining hope to rear
His darling children, loved and dear,
And clasp them to a mother's heart,
Feeling that they of him are part:
Back in their dear old Mentor home,
What feelings to their souls must come,
When they at eve are gathered there,
And gaze upon his vacant chair![1]
And then, perchance, his infant's tongue
Will stammer, "When will papa come?"
And quivering lips give faint reply,
While burning tears fill every eye;
And one — "his loved and petted child,"
His "Mollie dear" — with grief is wild![2]
And, oh! how many hearts draw nigh
To theirs in human sympathy!

The air is filled with mournful lamentation
    For our great Chieftain's fall!
The heartfelt tribute of a mighty nation,
    And sympathy from all!

[1] After the death of President Garfield, his wife and children returned to their home in Mentor, Ohio, which remained just as they left it
a few months before, when they went to reside at Washington. Their
feelings at the sight of each familiar object in their once happy home —
now made desolate by the loss of that dear husband and father — may
perhaps be imagined, but can never be described.

[2] President Garfield left five living children, — four sons, and one only
daughter, Mary, who, as such, was his petted child. She was fourteen
years old at his death. He called her by the pet name of "Mollie." She
was deeply affected by his sickness and sufferings, and overwhelmed
with grief at his untimely death.

From far-off lands, across the sobbing ocean,
  Comes many a kindly word :
The heart of England's Queen, with soft emotion
  And sympathy, is stirred.[1]

She sends kind greeting to a sister woman,
  Although to her unknown,
Showing that woman's heart is very human,
  Though mounted on a throne.

Oh, may it comfort their unbounded sorrow,
  And dry their tear-stained eyes !
The prostrate soul from sympathy will borrow,
  At times, new strength to rise.

The world is full of bleeding hearts, — and broken ;
  Some bleed and heal again ;
While some live on, and give no outward token ·
  Of their undying pain.

Not by the orphan's God are they unheeded :
  He heeds each sparrow's fall ;
The " balm in Gilead," when most sorely needed,
  He sendeth unto all.

[1] President Garfield's sufferings and death elicited many kind expres-
sions of sympathy and regret from the governments and crowned heads
of the Old World; and Queen Victoria sent more than one letter to Mrs.
Garfield, expressing, in the kindest manner, her sympathy and condo-
lence.

MINSTRELS AND MINSTRELSY OF THE MIDDLE AGES.

THE fine old German ballad, "The Minstrel's Curse," presents to the imagination a vivid picture of customs, personages, and rude events of the Middle Ages. It recounts, in sonorous and highly poetic language, the hard experience which the wandering minstrels of old sometimes met with, among the half-barbarous kings and barons of the warlike tribes of Scandinavia and Germany, in the rude and far-off ages now long since past and gone. And it tends to show how the rapt and inspired utterances of the bard or scald or minstrel were received as prophetic by the rude, credulous, and half-barbarous inhabitants of earth in those far-off, superstitious times. The minstrels (called in Germany "minne-singers") were a class of men peculiar to the Middle Ages, who united in themselves the arts of poetry and music; and they were accustomed to sing, to the accompaniment of the harp or lute or cithern, their own poetic compositions or the compositions of others.

They were called in Germany "minnesingers," from the ancient German word *minne*, which originally denoted love and friendship, — sometimes even divine love; and during the Middle Ages the German poets expressed by it particularly a pure, faithful, and generally happy love between the sexes. Love was the vital element of

22

chivalry; and, with the German poets, it was held to be something purer, more ideal, and more elevating, than among the French.

Thus the name of minnesingers was given to the German lyric poets of the Middle Ages, because love was the principal subject of their poems. These erotic poets (ἔρως, *love*) flourished in Germany for about two hundred years, — that is, from about 1150 to 1350, — and especially under the Suabian emperors of the house of Hohenstaufen, whence they were sometimes called the Suabian poets, and because the Suabian dialect prevailed in their poems. This same class of poets, during the Middle Ages, in the south of Europe, flourished extensively : and in France, Northern Italy, and parts of Spain, they were called trouveurs, trovéres, or troubadours, from the French word *trouver*, —" to find," " invent; " that is, they were the inventors, the makers, because they exercised the high and creative faculty of embodying sentiments and circumstances which had no existence except in their own imaginations, and, by their lofty and original poetic powers and creative faculties, they could impress the minds of their hearers with scenes and sentiments which often owed their reality of appearance only to the high creative art of the minstrel-poet. All these — the minstrels, minnesingers, trouveurs, or troubadours — seem to have been the genuine successors and inheritors of the ancient bards. " Bard " was the name that was given to the earliest poets of Greece, as well as to those inspired persons of the Celtic tribes of Western Europe, who, in the earliest times, raised the war-cry of their tribes in battle; and who, in times of peace, sang the exploits of their heroes, and celebrated the attributes of their gods, and chronicled the important events in the history of their tribes. The ancient bard was accustomed to deliver his rapt utterances in moments of high mental excitement, accompanied by the music of his harp or other musical instrument; and at such times he claimed to be inspired, and to speak and create things unknown to ordinary mortals: and this high creative faculty gained for him, in Greece, the appellation Ποιητής, "a maker," "creator"(of a poem), from the verb ποιέω, "I make," "produce," "create," "bring to pass." Strabo tells us that the ancient bards were treated with a respect approaching to veneration; and we learn from the histories of the earliest times, that among the Celtic tribes of Western Europe — especially in Wales, Ireland, and Scotland — the bards were looked upon as the natural priests, lawgivers, and heralds of the wild and barbarous tribes which occupied the ancient forests of those countries in the earliest times. And for centuries they were the honored companions and advisers of kings and princes, whose fame they have outlived; and some of their names are even celebrated at this late day. Among the earliest of the Welsh bards are Taliesin and Llywarch, who flourished during the sixth century: but their language is now nearly obsolete and forgotten; and the last echoes of their inspired harps, like those of their brother bards, have long since died away in the dim distance of forgotten time; and never, in all the coming ages of the future, shall their inspired tones be heard again, except it be in the faint and feeble echoes from out the dim past, which, in some rapt moments, reach and vibrate upon the intellectual tympanum of the poetic antiquary and scholar.

To the bards of pagan times, the minnesingers and

minstrels of the Middle Ages seem to be natural and genuine successors; and although, in the light of dawning
civilization and early Christianity, they were not accorded
all the distinctive qualities of inspiration and veneration
which had been given by the barbarians to the bards
of pagan times, still the minstrels of the Middle Ages
were looked upon generally as men of a superior order,
whose rapt vision could, in moments of poetic ecstasy,
pierce the dark curtain that conceals the future from
the eyes of ordinary mortals; and that to them, in their
ecstatic moments of mental inspiration, were yielded
glimpses into the dim future; and that to them sometimes —

"Coming events cast their shadows before."

The minstrels of the Middle Ages were generally of
noble descent, and the honored companions of kings,
princes, and nobles; and kings themselves sometimes
exercised the minstrel's art. It is well known to all
readers of history how Richard I. of England (Richard
Cœur de Lion) practiced the minstrel-art, and how (when
he had been cast into prison on his return from the Holy
Land through the dominions of the Duke of Austria) his
favorite minstrel, Blondel, in despair at his long absence,
set forth and wandered from castle to castle, found him
at last by means of singing, under the walls of his prison,
the minstrel-song which King Richard and he had for-
merly composed and sung together. This happened about
A.D. 1193. In the golden days of minstrelsy the minstrels usually dwelt as honored guests and companions in
the palaces and castles of kings and nobles, where their
society was much esteemed, because, by their songs and

harpings, they exalted and fostered the romantic and chivalric spirit of the times. But, in later times, as the minstrel-art declined with the decline of chivalry, the art of the minstrel came to be practiced by persons of less noble descent, who chanced to be endowed with high poetic talents. And then the minstrels often wandered from castle to castle, — like those in the ballad of " The Minstrel's Curse," — where they were usually honorably and kindly received; and where they sang their minstrel-songs, in old baronial halls, to the music of their harps, lutes, or citherns, for the amusement and diversion of listening lords and ladies, by whom they were admired in those rude times; and where they long supplied the want of needed entertainment; and where, it is to be hoped, for the sake of humanity's honor, as well as for the honor of chivalry and the profession of arms, they seldom or never received the harsh and bloody treatment that those poor minstrels met with, in the ballad, as a hard meed for all their golden songs, and in revenge for which the gray-haired old minstrel, pointing to the pale, disfigured countenance of his murdered son, utters — in the rapt ecstasy of poetic frenzy — " The Minstrel's Curse."

THE MINSTREL'S CURSE.

AN ANCIENT BALLAD.

(*From the German.*)

I.

THERE stood once in the olden time a castle high
    and grand :
Its lofty towers looked on the sea, and far upon the
    land ;
All round it fragrant gardens smiled, like garlands
    of rare worth,
Wherein, with rainbow-splendor, burst full many a
    fountain forth.

II.

In lands and conquests rich and proud, a king of
    ancient race
Once sat upon that castle's throne, with dark and
    faded face ;
His musings full of darksome fears, his looks were
    full of rage,
His every word was like a curse writ on a bloody
    page.

III.

Once journeyed towards that castle proud a noble
    minstrel-pair, —
The one with youthful golden locks, the other gray
    of hair:
The elder one, with noble harp, on gallant steed did
    ride;
The blooming youth, with active step, held ever by
    his side.

IV.

The elder minstrel, speaking, said, " Be ready now,
    my son!
Think of our noblest songs of love; sound every
    plaintive tone;
Exert thy soul to paint the power of pleasure and
    of pain;
Be it our aim to move with love the king's hard
    heart again."

V.

Now in the lofty-columned hall the minstrels ready
    stand,
With king and queen upon their thrones, and cour-
    tiers on each hand, —
The king in threatening splendor, like the flaming
    northern lights;
The queen as sweet and mild as the fair moon in
    summer nights.

VI.

The gray-haired minstrel swept the chords : 'twas
    wonderful to hear
How richer, ever richer, swelled their notes upon
    the ear ;
Then, with a heavenly sweetness, rose that younger
    minstrel's tones,
Joined by the deep voice of his sire, like mournful
    spirit-moans.

VII.

They sing of blessed golden times, of early love and
    spring ;
Of freedom, manly worth and truth and holiness,
    they sing ;
They sing of all the tender thoughts that soothe the
    heart to rest ;
They sing the high and noble deeds that thrill the
    human breast.

VIII.

That courtly throng around the king forgot all hate
    and scorn ;
The king's stern warriors bowed the head to God
    that summer morn ;
The sweet queen's tender heart was moved with sad-
    ness and with joy :
She cast the roses from her breast down to that
    minstrel-boy.

IX.

"Ye have misled my people, and allured my wife's
    weak choice,"
The raging king cried sternly out, with trembling
    limbs and voice.
Drawing his shining sword, he pierced that younger
    minstrel's breast :
Forth springs the blood-stream, and his golden
    songs are hushed to rest.

X.

Scattered is all that courtly throng. like leaves by
    autumn blast ;
And in his father's arms the dying minstrel breathed
    his last :
The father wrapped him in his cloak, and placed him
    on his steed ;
Holding him firmly there, he left that castle's court
    with speed.

XI.

The gray-haired minstrel halts beneath that portal-
    arch and wall,
And, seizing there his precious harp, — most price-
    less harp of all, —
Upon a marble column tall he dashed that harp's
    sweet chords,
And called till courts and castle all re-echoed with
    his words : —

XII.

" Woe to you and your lofty halls ! May never more
 be heard
Within these walls a harp's sweet tone, or song of
 minstrel-bard !
Oh, here be only sighs and groans, and timid slave-
 steps old !
Avenging ghosts you and your walls tread down to
 dust and mould !

XIII.

" Woe to you and your gardens sweet here in the
 fair May-light !
I show you here this dead one's face, this pale disfigured sight,
That ye thereat may wither, and these fountains
 cease to play !
That, petrified and perished. ye shall lie in future
 day !

XIV.

" Woe to thee, cursed murderer ! thou curse of minstrelsie !
Thy strivings after crowns of bloody fame in vain
 shall be ;
Thy name shall be forgotten, and in endless night
 go out ;
And thou shalt be like dying groan in empty air
 breathed out ! "

XV.

The old man's curse is spoken now, and Heaven
    has heard his prayer :
That lofty castle's walls lie low ; its ruined halls are
    bare.
One lofty column only tells of splendor past and
    gone,
And that — already thunder-riven — shall soon be
    lying prone.

XVI.

Instead of fragrant gardens there, are desolate
    heath-lands ;
No tree now scatters grateful shade, no fountains
    cool the sands.
Of that king's name, no hero-book[1] or song gives
    any word :
Sunk and forgotten, all are lost ! — the minstrel's
    curse was heard !

---

[1] Hero-book; i.e., the German "Heldenbuch," or "Book of Heroes."
The "Heldenbuch" is a very celebrated collection of old German poems,
in which are embodied many national traditions of Germany in very
remote times, and wherein are recorded in song the exploits and adventures of the most celebrated knights and heroes of Germany.

These poems have become world-renowned, and interest and excite
the imagination, not only from their antiquity and rude poetic beauties,
but also by their vivid and romantic tales of love and war in the olden
times, when love and war were almost the only occupations of knights,
nobles, and heroes; and for a knight or king not to be honorably men-
tioned in song and hero-book, was simply to be consigned to a nameless
and dishonorable grave. The poems of which the "Heldenbuch" is
composed were written by the earliest poets of Germany, who, like the

ancient minstrels of England and Scotland, probably wandered from castle to castle, and sang them to the accompaniment of the harp or cithern, in old baronial halls, to delighted audiences of lords and ladies. These poems were composed by various authors at different times, and were afterwards collected together into a sort of continuous history, as the Iliad is said to have been in Greece. Many of them relate to the Suabian period; and they, together with the "Nibelungen Lied,"—another very celebrated collection of German national songs, about which Mr. Carlyle wrote much,—are to Germany what the Iliad of Homer is to Greece; and, indeed, the "Nibelungen Lied" is often called the German Iliad. These old heroic poems, says Mr. Carlyle, "are strangely intertwisted, and growing out of and into one another; and they show to the Germans that they too, as well as the Greeks, have their heroic age; and round the old Valhalla, as their northern Pantheon, are grouped a world of demi-gods and wonders. . . . A strange charm lies in these old tones [songs], where, in gay dancing melodies, the sternest tidings are sung to us; and deep floods of sadness and strife play lightly in little curling billows, like seas in summer."

MIGNON.

MIGNON is one of the sweet and interesting characters
— perhaps the most interesting — in Göthe's " Wilhelm
Meister." In her earliest childhood — of which she still
retains some faint and imperfect memories — she had
been stolen from her noble home and parents by a band
of strolling gipsies or jugglers, and secretly carried from
her own sunny Italy, across the Alps, into Germany. As
she grew up she was taught by her harsh masters to
sing, dance, and perform feats on the rope, etc., to gain
money for those who had stolen her. But, through all
her hardships, she still retained a faint remembrance of
her early, happy childhood in a beautiful home in warm
and sunny Italy, — where she had been loved and petted,
— with a deep and longing desire to return thither again.
And she remembered more vividly her sad and dark journey over the dangerous and fearful Alps, with their misty
cloud-paths and dreadful avalanches, which had probably
filled her childish and terror-stricken mind with horror.
Wilhelm Meister happened one day to witness the per-
formances of Mignon and her *troupe*, during which
Mignon was unmercifully abused. This so aroused his
sympathy for the child, that he obtained possession of
her, and became her protector. One morning, soon after,
he was surprised at finding her before his door singing
the following song to the accompaniment of a cithern,

34

which had accidentally fallen into her hands. On finishing the song for the second time, she stood silent for a moment, looked keenly into Wilhelm's face, and asked him, "Know'st thou the land?" — "It must be Italy," said Wilhelm, musingly ; but the child's history was yet a mystery to him. "Where didst thou get the little song?" said he. "Italy," said Mignon, with a sad and earnest air: "if thou go to Italy, take me along with thee, for I am too cold here." — "Hast thou been there already, little dear?" said Wilhelm. But the child was silent, and nothing more could he learn from her.

MIGNON.

(From the German.)

I.

Know'st thou the land where the fair citrons grow? —
Through foliage dark golden oranges glow, —
Where the blue heavens breathe fragrant, balmy air,
And modest myrtle stands with laurel fair?
  Know'st thou it well? then thither, oh!
  Would I with thee, my own beloved one, go!

II.

Know'st thou the house, with columns ranged around?
The great hall shines; the rooms with gilt abound;
And marble statues stand and gaze on me,
And say, "Poor child, what have they done to
  thee?"
  Know'st thou it well? then thither, oh!
  Would I with thee, my dear protector, go!

36

III.

Know'st thou the mountain where the cloud-paths
     stray?
The muleteer seeks in mist his doubtful way;
In the deep cavern dwells the dragon's brood;
Down plunge the rocks, and over them the flood.
     Know'st thou it well? then thither, oh!
     Goes our own way! O father, let us go!

THE MAIDEN'S LAMENT.

(From the German.)

I.

THE oak forests roar,
 And the dark clouds sail by ;
On the green of the shore
 Sits a maiden to sigh ;
And the wild waves are breaking with power and
 might,
While the maiden sighs out in the dark, gloomy
 night,
 And her eyes are all reddened with weeping.

II.

The heart sad and broken ;
 Life, empty and vain,
Now gives her no token
 Or comfort in pain :
" Thou Holy One, call now thy child back again !
I have tasted earth's pleasures ; no more now re-
 main :
 I have lived, and loved one who is sleeping."

38

III.

But the course of her tears
    Is all fruitless and vain ;
The lamenting for years
    Wakes the dead not again.
Oh ! tell what can comfort and heal the sick heart
When sweet vanished love leaves us only its smart :
    I, the heavenly one, will not deny it.

IV.

Let in vain be the course
    Of the tears that are shed ;
Let laments have no force
    To awaken the dead ;
Still the sweetest of pleasure for hearts that must
    mourn,
When love's vanished pleasure no more can return,
    Is love's hallowed grief.   All must try it.

MAN.

(*From the German.*)

I.

In the world, outcast and lonely,
  Stands weak man, forsaken here,
Storms and winds around him raging;
  Nothing to his heart is dear.

II.

Lovingly the stars call to him,
  And the sweet flowers whisper, too,
" Look not sadly on the future,
  We, O man, are one with you! "

III.

And he presses, with deep longing,
  Earth and heaven to his heart;
And, in warm and tender tear-drops,
  Love relieves his keenest smart.

40

IV.

But the north-wind sweeps the meadows ;
    All the flowerets fade and die ;
While, with pilgrim-staff, he wanders
    Earth, and puts his trust on high.

V.

And, with heart and soul still hoping,
    Looks he to heaven's starry train ;
And the tender blossoms, bursting
    From the bleak earth, bloom again.

VI.

Youth's companions, from him fleeing,
    Give him o'er to want and pain ;
No one sharing now his sorrows,
    Old age weighs him down amain.

VII.

Lastly, seeks he for the threshold
    Where his cradle once did stand ;
But the place is strange and altered :
    No one takes him by the hand.

VIII.

Trustingly he gazes upwards
    To the heavens, as once before :
" Oh ! my course on earth is ended ;
    Youth to me will come no more.

IX.

" Many things with time may perish ;
 Still some must immortal be :
One there is, — and I will trust Him, —
 One, whom those bright stars can see !

X.

" I can love, believing, hoping :
 Through the darkness shines a light,
And I see the heavens opening
 When breaks the heart in endless night."

OF US THERE ARE SEVEN.

(From the German.)

I.

SURROUNDED with fair flowers, sat a child beside a
grave,
Where in the morning wind her long, dark flowing
hair did wave :
Her cheeks were glowing fresh and fair, like cherries
in sweet May ;
Her fair eyes beaming clear and bright, like stars at
close of day.

II.

Never was bird more lovely seen that in the
branches sings ;
Never gazelle more joyful was that through the
greenwood springs :
" Of brothers and of sisters dear, how many are ye,
pray ? "
" Seven in all there are of us," the child did quickly
say.

III.

"Two planting in the garden are ; two sleep in
    green graves here ;
And two are fishing on the lake ; seven are we, sir,
    'tis clear ! "
" If two are fishing on the lake, and in the garden
    two,
Then are ye certainly not seven : my darling child,
    speak true ! "

IV.

" Yes, two of us are sleeping in these little green
    graves here :
Therefore we surely seven are, — yes, seven, sir, 'tis
    clear ! "
" If two of you lie buried here beneath these
    flowerets wild,
Then are ye surely only five, my good and darling
    child ! "

V.

"Oh, no ! oh, no ! not five, kind sir ! seven, cer-
    tainly, are we ;
For brother dear, and sister dear, come often back
    to me !
Oh, long and patiently lay sister dear with failing
    breath,
And smiled upon us tenderly, as closed her eyes in
    death.

VI.

" She taught me often of God's love, to turn my
 thoughts from vice,
Till God called her unto himself to dwell in Para-
 dise ;
Then came I often to her grave — I and my brother
 dear —
To cover it with fragrant flowers, and sit beside her
 here.

VII.

" But when cold Winter killed the flowers, and the
 white snow was here,
Then God called little brother, too, to dwell with
 sister dear :
Now I come here to deck their graves with flowers
 red and white,
And knit, and pray, and eat my evening meals in
 the twilight.

VIII.

" And oft, when weary by this cross I lie in slumbers light,
Then come they down from heaven in forms all
 wonderfully bright :
They leave beside me heavenly flowers that in God's
 garden grow,
Where with the pure white lambs of God the shining angels go.

IX.

"Oh, gladly would I there remain ; but, vanishing,
    they say,
'Be brave, dear sister, till we meet again some
    future day ! '
Therefore not five, but seven, sir, in all, are we, 'tis
    clear, —
In garden and upon the lake, and in these green
    graves here."

THE RICHEST PRINCE.

(From the German.

I.

LOUDLY praising — in fine speeches —
 Their rich countries, great and small,
Once sat many German princes
 In Worms' high imperial hall.

II.

Proudly spake the King of Saxons :
 " Richest land?   Why, that is mine !
Endless treasures, in her mountains
 Buried, lie in many a mine."

III.

" See my land in rich abundance ! "
 Cried the proud Prince of the Rhine :
" Golden harvests fill her valleys ;
 On her hills, rich grapes for wine."

47

IV.

"Mighty cities and rich convents"—
Ludwig, King of Baiern,[1] said—
"Cause my land of all your vaunted
Treasures not to stand in dread."[2]

V.

Eberhard,—he of the dark beard,—
Wurtemberg's belovèd lord,
Said, "My land has but small cities,
And her hills no silver hoard.

VI.

"But she holds one hidden treasure,—
In all kingdoms none so great,—
I can lay my head with safety
In each lap within my State!"

VII.

"Then," cried out the Prince of Saxons,
King of Baiern, Lord of Rhine,
"Bearded count, thou art the richest!
No land can compare with thine."

[1] Bavaria.
[2] „Schaffen daß mein Land den euren
Wohl nicht steht an Schäßen nach."

THE TWO LITTLE WINDOWS.

(*From the German.*)

I.

THERE is a grand and stately house,
  With but two windows small;
And through them all the world looks in,
  From out them one sees all.

II.

And ever there a painter sits
  Who knows his art all through;
And he paints all things rapidly, —
  White, black, red, green, and blue.

III.

He paints things square, round, short, or long,
  As he the fancy takes;
And no one could name half the shades
  And forms which there he makes.

IV.

He's a magician, I aver,
  Who can earth's secrets see,
And paint them on a little spot
  No larger than a pea!

V.

What that house's lord implores or thinks,
  On those two panes paints he;
So that each one who passes by
  It plainly there can see.

VI.

If that house's lord at home is gay,
  Or if he suffers pain,
Then pearly drops oft show themselves
  Upon each little pane.

VII.

In pleasant weather, sunny days,
  Then are they clear and bright;
But if it freezes, storms, and snows,
  Then darkened is their light.

VIII.

And, when that house's lord goes to rest,
  No light he needs to take;
For then Death slams the shutters to,
  And, oh! the windows break!

CRADLE SONG.

(From the German.)

I.

Sleep, my heart's treasure ! My darling art thou !
Close thy sweet blue eyes in soft slumber now ;
All is as quiet and still as the grave :
Sleep while I watch, and the flies from thee wave.

II.

Now is thy golden time, free from all pain :
Later, oh, later is never the same ;
Once, by thy couch, let care place itself here :
Ne'er wilt thou slumber so sweetly, my dear.

III.

Angels from heaven, as lovely as thou,
Hover around thee, and smile on thee now :
Later, indeed, they may come to thee here,
But only to wipe away many a tear.

51

IV.

Sleep, my heart's treasure! Come night when it will,
Mother sits by thee and watches thee still!
Be it late, be it early, — however time flies, —
Mother's love, darling, ne'er slumbers or dies!

THE CASTLE BY THE SEA.

(From the German.)

I.

" HAST thou seen that stately castle
    Standing by the moaning sea?
Golden, rose-tinged clouds hang o'er it,
    Moving there mysteriously.

II.

" Seemingly it would plunge downward
    Through the clear flood at its base,
Or would struggle and mount upward
    Where the red clouds glow in space."

III.

" Yes, indeed, I well have seen it,
    That high castle by the sea,
And the round moon o'er it sailing
    Through the mists mysteriously."

IV.

" And the wind's and sea's low moaning,
  Gave they not a wondrous sound?
Heard'st thou from those halls of grandeur
  Tuneful harps and songs resound?"

V.

" All the winds and all the wavelets,
  They were hushed in quiet rest:
Mourning songs, from that proud castle,
  Heard I there, with tears oppressed."

VI.

" Saw'st thou, moving through that castle,
  The proud king and stately queen?
Saw'st thou waving of red mantles,
  Or of golden crowns the sheen?

VII.

" With delight, were they not leading
  A young maiden sweet and rare,
Radiant as the beams of morning,
  In her golden tresses fair?"

VIII.

" Ay, indeed, I saw the parents;
  But no shining crowns were there:
They were in black mourning-garments;
  But no maiden saw I there!"

THE MINSTREL.

(*From the German.*)

The following exquisite ballad is from the German of Göthe. It very happily exemplifies some of the genuine characteristics of the true ballad style, in which the poet often gives us general outlines of the story and events to be related, leaving it to the reader's own imagination to supply and fill in all that is left unexpressed; while the poet, with effective brevity of expression and great boldness of transition from thought to thought, projects his rapidly succeeding poetic pictures upon the mental canvas of the reader's mind in concise, and often very elliptical, sentences.

I.

" What hear I by our castle-gate?
    What notes upon the drawbridge ring?
Doth there some wandering minstrel wait
    Before us in our hall to sing? "
Thus spake the king.   His page ran out,
    And soon returned, with joyous shout,
Leading a gray-haired minstrel in.

II.

" Hail, noble king and lords ! " he cried ;
    " Hail, ladies fair of high degree !
Oh, what a heaven ! stars side by side !
    Who knows what all their names may be?

55

In lordly hall, where splendors shine,
  Be closed mine eyes: here is no time
With wondering delight to gaze."

III.

The minstrel closed his wondering eyes,
  And swept the sounding chords along:
Bold knights beheld, with deep surprise;
  Fair dames, with bowed head, heard the song;
The king, well pleasèd with his strain,
  Would give the minstrel golden chain
As guerdon for his minstrelsie.

IV.

" Oh, give to me no golden chains:
  Let them to thy bold knights be given,
By whose brave arms, on battle-plains,
  Thine enemy's array is riven;
Or on thy chancellor bestow,
  And let him still the golden show
With other weighty burdens bear.

V.

" I sing, as sings the summer bird
  Whose home is in the greenwood tree:
The songs, from mine own bosom poured,
  Are rich rewards, — enough for me;

But, might I claim one gift as mine,
Then be one draught of noblest wine
  To me in golden goblet given."

VI.

He took the wine ; he drank it all :
  " O draught as sweet as light from heaven !
Oh, happy be the princely hall
  Where such sweet gifts are freely given !
While well ye fare, oh, think of me !
  And thank God freely, as I ye,
For this rich draught of wine, now thank."

I THINK OF THEE.

(From the German.)

I.

I EVER think of thee
When through the greenwood tree
The nightingale's sweet note
Is poured from muffled throat:
   When thinkest thou of me?

II.

I ever think of thee
Where in the glow I see
The evening shades appear,
By shady fountains clear:
   Where thinkest thou of me?

III.

I ever think of thee,
With kind thoughts, painfully,
While longing anxiously,
With warm tears flowing free:
   How thinkest thou of me?

58

IV.

Oh, dearest! think of me
Until I meet with thee
Upon that better star;
And, be I near or far,
    I'll ever think of thee.

THE CASTLE OF BONCOURT.

(From the German.)

This pathetic little ballad is from the German of Adalbert de Chamisso, a naturalist and poet of considerable note, who circumnavigated the globe. The Castle of Boncourt, in Champagne, France, was long the family residence of Chamisso's ancestors, who ranked among the first families of France, and at the Castle of Boncourt Chamisso was born in 1781; but during the great Revolution the castle was assailed, and razed to the ground; and the impoverished family, with the boy Chamisso, fled to Germany. Knowing the history of the author's life, we can the better appreciate the sweetness and beauty of the sentiments in these touching memories of his childhood, when, in the reveries of age, he beholds, in imagination, the obliterated castle of his fathers again all perfect, as he had known it in his youth.

I.

In dreams I go back to my childhood,
　And bow down my head in deep pain :
O visions of youth long forgotten !
　How comes it ye seek me again?

II.

From shady inclosures, high rising,
　I see a grand castle of state :
Those battlements — towers — well I know them ;
　That bridge of dark stone, and that gate.

60

III.

And from that escutcheon all sadly
    The lions look down upon me;
Their faces familiar, I greet them,
    And hasten the courtyard to see.

IV.

The sphinx still lies there by the fountain,
    And there is the fig-tree still green;
And there are the windows and chamber,
    Where first I dreamed out life's young dream

V.

I seek, in the old castle-chapel,
    The graves which my ancestors fill:
Behold them, where from lofty columns
    Their noble escutcheons hang still!

VI.

Not well can my dim eyes decipher
    The inscriptions in characters dim,
Though clearly, through richly stained windows
    The light from above them shines in.

VII.

Thus stands, of my fathers, the castle
    In memory's land firm and good,
Though, truly, from earth it has vanished,
    And plows turn the ground where it stood.

VIII.

Be fruitful, O fields of my fathers !
  I bless you, though deep is my pain,
And bless whomsoever is guiding
  The plow on my ancestral plain.

IX.

But I — I will quickly arouse me,
  And, with my loved harp in my hand,
Will wander the wide world all over,
  While singing from land unto land.

EARLY BALLAD-POETRY OF DIFFERENT NATIONS.

He who said, "Let me make a nation's ballads, and I care not who makes her laws," was wiser than he even dreamed of being; for many an old ballad, upon some touching and popular theme, will live, and bear its "maker's" name to future ages, when the nation, as such, with all its laws, has ceased to exist for ever. The word "ballad," we are told, is akin to "ballet;" being derived from the Greek βάλλειν, "to throw or move rapidly," and may indicate that the "makers" and singers of the first rude rhymes among ancient nations were in the habit of dancing while they sang, as a forcible illustration to these early songs.

The word "ballad"—meaning "a short epic poem"— is from the Italian *ballata*, which was used to express an old kind of song of a lyric nature; and *ballata* is derived from the Italian verb *ballare*, "to dance." Now this word *ballata* was borrowed from the Italians by the troubadours, or minstrel-poets of Provence; and, by the Norman poets, it was carried northward in Europe, as well as into England and Scotland, being applied by them all to those short heroic poems and love-songs which were composed to celebrate the deeds of their heroes, and recount the adventures and passions of knights and lovers.

All the Scandinavian nations took great delight in this species of poetry; and their minstrel-poets often celebrated the deeds of heroes, and the passions and adventures of lovers, in these short epic songs or ballads. Although the name "ballad" has an Italian origin, still that species of poetry never flourished to any great extent in Italy; for Italian poetry has, on the other hand, always retained a certain classical spirit of antiquity. It seems to be conceded by some of the best authors upon the subject, that the species of poetry which we now understand by the word "ballad" is of Teutonic origin; and yet, in the south of Europe, the Spaniards have a species of songs or ballads of great excellence and beauty, and which appear to be at least of equal antiquity with the ballads of Northern nations.

The early home of the English ballad seems to have been in "the North Countrie," — that is, in the northern parts of England and the south of Scotland ; and, even after the Conquest, the Normans who settled there, and who did not understand the language of the native bards, and therefore affected to despise it, left it to the common people, among whom the native songs and ballads long flourished, and retained their popular character and simplicity.[1]

Later, indeed, the feudal wars of the Norman knights, and their chivalric spirit, gave new subjects to the ballad-

---

[1] After the Norman Conquest, the king and great lords and barons made an effort to extirpate the English language, and to substitute the Norman French among the conquered people; and, to aid this project, it was ordered that all legal proceedings should be carried on in French, and that the records of the courts of law should be kept in the same language. But neither the influence of the great lords, — in whose petty

poetry of the country, and contributed to modify its character. The former bards gradually became minstrels, who attached themselves to the great lords and knights, and, composing songs in honor of their exploits, waited upon them, and devoted themselves to their amusement, receiving from them pecuniary rewards and hospitality. In ancient times the ballad seems not to have been so popular with the people in Germany as it was in England and Scotland; but in more modern times the German ballads are often accounted the best, and some of the greatest of the poets of Germany have indulged in their composition, — such as Göthe, Schiller, Bürger, Uhland, Schreiber, Kerner, and many others.

But in exquisite and delicious ballad-poetry there is no country in all Europe that can surpass sunny, romantic Spain, that land of serenade and song, of haughty dons and dark-eyed donnas; the land of chivalry, romance, and love; the land alternately of Christians and of Moors; and in this same sunny land of Spain are to be found the richest stores of ancient ballad-poetry.

It has well been said that those who have the making of a nation's ballads can well dispense with the honor of making her laws: for a nation's laws are but ephemeral indeed in comparison to the duration of a nation's ballads; and to their ballad-poetry are all nations greatly indebted for the preservation of a knowledge of their ancient manners and customs, and, in the earliest times,

courts French was exclusively spoken, — nor the authority of the king, even, could change the language of an entire people; and, after it had been tried about three hundred years, the attempt was given up, and since that time English has been the language of the law-courts as well as of the people at large. Some French words are, however, retained in legal phraseology.

for the preservation even of their most important historical events.

Where, for instance, can be found to-day so true a picture of the manners and customs of the Greeks and Trojans of three thousand years ago as in the poems of Homer ? — "the blind old bard of Scio's rocky isle !" who, as has been maintained, was probably only a wandering singer, a bard, a minstrel, a troubadour of prehistoric times; who, it has been suggested, collected the most important ballads of his own and previous times, and, by creations and additions of his own, wove them into a sort of continuous history of the great events that stirred the world of Greece and Asia Minor more than a thousand years before the birth of Christ; doing in the East what (more than a thousand years afterwards) another blind old bard did for the West, when Ossian — the rhapsodist, the minstrel, the great troubadour of the Gaelic tribes of the Western world — sang the historic deeds of his own and former times in the pure, classic strains of his own bold and figurative Gaelic tongue, — a language as pure, as poetical, and as rich in compound epithets and startling metaphor, as that in which the Grecian bard of old sang his undying strains to the ravished ears of all the world for all time to come. And so we owe a debt of gratitude and love to the bards and minstrels of all times and tongues; for, long before the days of authentic history, the bards and minstrels of all nations wove the important events of their own times into short rhythmical histories, which were handed down from generation to generation, often perhaps undergoing some slight changes in the oral transmission, but, in the main, true (in most cases at least) to the facts and customs of the ages now gone by. And, as meter was the form of language best adapted to the oral transmission of passing events, it was natural that poetry, in the literary history of all nations, should have an earlier origin than prose; and, even in a low state of social and literary advancement, the art of poetry might attain, in the keeping of the bards, to a considerable degree of excellence, and even to a lofty elevation of thought and language. Such, indeed, is the case with the poetry of Ossian; for in his works there is a great degree of regularity and poetic art, wherein the deepest tenderness and delicacy of sentiment are often found, as well as the fire and enthusiasm which belong to bards of the earliest times.

The Goths — under which name are comprehended all the ancient Scandinavian tribes — were a fierce and warlike people, and not noted for a knowledge of the liberal arts; and yet they had their bards and their songs from the most remote times, — songs which recounted the deeds of their heroes, and the traditions of their countries and tribes. And many of those ancient songs, called *vyses,* were found engraven upon the rocks, "in a sort of Runic rhyme," cut there by the poets of the Scandinavian tribes, who were called *scalders,* in the ancient Runic characters of the times; and the more ancient the songs of the scalders, says Dr. Percy, the more they were believed to be connected with true history. There is a very curious specimen of the poetry of the scalders preserved by Olaus Wormius, a learned Dane, who was skilled in the antiquities of Denmark and Norway. This literary curiosity is preserved in his work, " De Literatura Runica." The specimen here

meant is the *epicedium*, or funeral song, which was
composed by King Regner Lodbrog of Denmark. This
Lodbrog was a celebrated warrior of the piratical class
in the eighth century, who had the misfortune to finally
fall into the power of his enemy, by whom he was imprisoned, and condemned to death. Being a celebrated
scalder, he consoled himself in prison by composing this
epicedium, or funeral song, in which he recounted the
warlike exploits of his early life, and declared the forti-
tude with which he should meet death, and his hopes
and expectations of an exalted and happy position in
the halls of Odin, saying, "In the house of the mighty
Odin no brave man laments death. I come not with the
voice of despair to Odin's hall." The entire composition
is a remarkable and curious specimen of the customs and
feelings predominant among men in those far-off ages,
and of the poetic attainments of those times. What the
scalders were to the ancient Scandinavians, the bards
were to the ancient Britons and Celts. The Celtæ were
a numerous and warlike people, distinct from the Goths
and Teutons, who, in the earliest times, held dominion
over a large portion of Western Europe, and established
themselves firmly in ancient Gaul ; and, among the
Celtæ or Gauls, there were found, from the earliest
times, two orders of men, who were held in the highest
estimation. These were the druids, who were their
philosophers and priests, and, to some extent, their lawgivers; and the bards, whose office it was to compose
songs in honor of the heroic deeds of great chieftains
and in celebration of important events, and to recite
them to the assembled people on public occasions. The
druids dwelt together in societies; and, philosophizing

upon the destiny of man, they asserted the immortality of the human soul. The bards, in their character of poets and historians of their people, — among whom the office was hereditary, — came to be so numerous, that every chieftain of note was accustomed to have his own particular bard, who was considered a member of his household, and held a position of importance in his little court. On all important occasions the bards were messengers between contending tribes, and ambassadors between the courts of princes and chieftains. Their persons were held sacred upon all occasions; for, as says Ossian, "though the soul of Cairbar was dark, he feared to stretch his sword to the bards." "Loose the bards: they are the sons of other times ; their voices shall be heard in other ages, when the kings of Temora have failed." Thus the Celtic nations of remote times had their bards, to whom the minstrels of the Middle Ages seem to have been the genuine successors; and the Gothic nations of earliest ages had their scalds, or scalders (smoothers or polishers of language), to whom succeeded the minnesingers of the Middle Ages throughout Germany: but there was, in the south of Europe, one nation whose poetry in its early stages was, for hundreds of years, tinged by lasting influences from another quarter of the globe. That country was Spain, which, as has already been stated, is unsurpassed by any country in Europe in the rich stores of its ballad-poetry; but the character of that poetry was early tinged by Oriental influences.

In order fully to understand the reasons for this, it is necessary to look, for a moment, at the physical features and geographical situation of the peninsula of Spain, and to take into consideration the characters of the different peoples who contributed to make up its ancient inhabitants. Spain, including Portugal, is surrounded on three sides by the Mediterranean Sea and Atlantic Ocean; while more than one-half of its northern portion is washed by the Bay of Biscay, and its remaining part is separated from the rest of Europe by the lofty chain of the Pyrenees Mountains, thus rendering it, in ancient times, more isolated than other European countries.

Spain was anciently called Iberia; and the ancient Iberians, who had been driven towards the West, formed the basis of the population of Spain, including ancient Lusitania (now Portugal). Their original language is said to still exist in the Basque. Later still came in the Celtæ, who were mingled to some extent with them. Thus the Spanish people were descended from Iberians and Celts, somewhat mingled with Carthaginian and Roman colonists; for, as early as the third century before the Christian era, Rome and Carthage contended for the possession of the Spanish peninsula.[1] Later still, after a struggle of near two hundred years, Agrippa, the general of Augustus, overcame the Spanish inhabitants, and

---

[1] In the primitive ages the different tribes of men were named from some characteristic of the people, or from the place of their residence. Thus, to the primitive inhabitants of the west of Europe the Greeks gave the name of Κελτοι, i.e., Celts, —a word which signified *woodsmen.* These were said to be descended from the same ancestors as the Greeks and Romans, but they had early migrated into Gaul and Spain; and the primitive occupiers of these countries had been pushed forward, by successive hordes of men, till they were stopped by the ocean or impassable mountain-chains, and there their descendants are at present to be found. And, of these, are a part of the inhabitants of the north of Spain, with those of France south of the River Garonne, called by the Romans *Garumna flumen,* and the inhabitants they called Aquitani and Cantabri; but more modern historians called them Cantabrians, Gascoigns, and Basques, and these still retain their ancient native language.

Spain was subjected to the Roman power; and Augustus himself founded the colony of Cæsar Augusta (Saragossa), and for nearly four hundred years the Roman language and manners prevailed in the peninsula. After the irruption of the barbarians into the Roman Empire, the Vandals, Suevi, and Alans spread themselves over the Spanish peninsula. In the fifth century Wallia founded, in Spain, the kingdom of the Visigoths; and the Vandals, from whom Andalusia received its name, withdrew into Africa. In the latter part of the fifth century the great Euric extended the kingdom of the Visigoths in Spain, and, driving out the Romans, gave them their first written laws. Nearly a hundred years later, Leowigild overturned the kingdom of the Suevi in Galicia; and his successor introduced the Catholic religion about A.D. 586, and that, in time, gave the corrupt Latin language a predominance over the Gothic.

The Romans called that part of Western Africa which lies opposite to Spain, Mauritania; and the inhabitants thereof they called Moors. This territory of Mauritania was long under the dominion of the Vandals, who had established there, at one time, a powerful kingdom, which was, however, overthrown in the first half of the sixth century. During the seventh century the Saracens (Arabians), who were followers of Mohammed, extended their conquests over this part of Africa from the East, and Mauritania came to be governed by a deputy of the Caliph of Damascus. The Saracens, or Arabians, being firmly established and powerful in Mauritania, opposite to the Spanish peninsula, they, in the beginning of the eighth century, took advantage of the disorders of the Visigoths in Spain, and reduced a large

part of the peninsula under their yoke, holding it in subjection for nearly eight hundred years thereafter, with
the exception of some of the northern provinces and portions of the sea-coast; and thus the greater part of Spain
was for a time a province of the caliphs of Bagdad.

But, the power of the caliphs declining in time, the
different governors became after a while independent,
and assumed the title of kings; and Arabian princes
reigned at Saragossa, Toledo, Valencia, and Seville; and
the Moorish language and customs became almost universal where the Arabians held sway.

Meanwhile the Visigoths long and steadily maintained
their freedom in the mountainous districts of the north,
until the Moorish dynasties became weakened by ages of
dissensions; and then the Christian kings wrested one
portion of the country after another from their Arabian
conquerors, until only the Moorish kingdom of Granada
remained to them; and that was obliged to acknowledge
the Castilian supremacy, and was finally conquered by
Ferdinand and Isabella A.D. 1491; and the Moorish
dominion in Spain was ended, after nearly eight hundred
years of duration. The Spanish writers gave the name
of Moors to their Arabian conquerors, on account of their
former residence in Mauritania; but during the dominion
of the Moors in Spain, and while the rest of Europe was
steeped in barbarism, learning and the arts flourished
with unusual glory among the polished and learned
Arabians in the Spanish peninsula. The universities
and libraries which they established and maintained at
Cordova ("the Delphi of the peninsula") and other
places, were resorted to, even by Christians, as the seat
of Greco-Arabic literature, where the Aristotelian phil-

osophy was taught by Arabian scholars of the most profound learning; and it is even said that Europe received from them the knowledge of the present arithmetical characters,[1] as well as much other useful knowledge.

Thus it will be seen that the Spanish people of the Middle Ages were descended from ancient Iberians, Celts, Carthaginians, Romans, Vandals, and Visigoths, whose peculiarities were all heightened and tinged by Oriental influences during their hundreds of years of mixture and intercourse with the Arabians, or Moors, who were a polished, gallant, and chivalrous people.

The oldest language in all Spain was that of the ancient Cantabrians,[2] the bravest and rudest of the

---

[1] The learned Arabians brought the science of algebra with them from the East, and first introduced it into Spain, whence it was carried into other European countries. The oldest known work upon the science of algebra which we possess is said to be the one by Diophantus of Alexandria, a geometrician who is supposed to have lived in the fourth century: but the science is of Oriental discovery, as its name — from the Arabic, *al gabron* — plainly indicates; and Europe is indebted to the learned Arabians, who brought it into Spain, for its first acquaintance with this wonderful and useful science, as well as for much other useful and curious knowledge.

[2] The Cantabrian, which is also called the Basque, language — spoken by the inhabitants of the Pyrenees — is one of the purest specimens of the original language of the ancient Κελτοι, or Celts. They were the primitive inhabitants of the west of Europe. The Basque and the Hiberno-Celtic, or primitive language of Ireland, with the Gaelic, or native language of the Highlanders of Scotland, are said to be the purest remains of the ancient Celtic language now in existence; and they are almost the only ones: between the Hiberno-Celtic and the Scottish Gaelic, when correctly written, there is really but very little difference. The language of the Welsh, who were descended from the Cimbri, or primitive inhabitants of Jutland, is said to bear a strong resemblance to the Celtic; and also the Armoric, spoken by the descendants of the primitive inhabitants of Brittany, in France, is said to be of Celtic origin. There was once a language called the Cornish, which

Iberian tribes who inhabited ancient Hispania. They
were the descendants of the primitive inhabitants of the
northern mountains of Spain; and their language is said
to exist still in the Basque language, spoken by the
people of the Pyrenees. To this were added Phœnician
and Carthaginian words, and the whole was modified
by the Latin during the sway of the Romans;[1] while,
under the Visigoths, there was developed a dialect which
was called the *Romanzo*, or Romance language, which
seems to have been more or less mixed with the Latin
down to the time of the Moorish invasion. When the
Moors had conquered a large part of Spain, their dialect
— a fine one, and much cultivated in poetry — was
adopted, and soon spoken with fluency, by the people in
all parts of the peninsula where the Moors held sway.

was also of Celtic origin: it was spoken by the ancient inhabitants of
the county of Cornwall, in the extreme south-west corner of England;
but it has now passed out of existence.

[1] The modern Spanish and Portuguese, as well as the modern French
and Italian, are composed to a large extent of Latin words, many of
which are derived from the Greek; but they are generally much changed
in their orthography, as well as in their inflections. Many of them were
borrowed from the Greek by the Romans, and by them carried into
Gaul, and there naturalized during the five or six hundred years that
the Romans held sway; and, as they held Spain in subjection even
longer, they firmly established a large percentage of Latin words in the
Spanish. Still the Spanish and Portuguese, as well as the French and
Italian, retained many of their original Celtic words. But it must be
remembered that the Spanish and Portuguese contain, moreover, many
words which were introduced by Carthaginian colonists long before
Spain came under the Roman sway, as well as many which were afterwards brought in by the Arabians, or Moors, who held the greater part
of the peninsula in subjection for hundreds of years long after the Roman
sway; and the Goths, who drove out the Romans, also introduced into
the Spanish very many words of Gothic origin.

But the descendants of the Visigoths retired before the conquering Moors to the northern and mountainous portions of the peninsula, and along the shores of the Atlantic, where several small kingdoms or principalities were formed, which were more or less united in their long struggles against their common enemy. This division of the old inhabitants into several small kingdoms had its influence upon the Spanish language; for there were as many dialects of the Spanish Romanzo as there were kingdoms ; but these dialects gradually blended with each other as the kingdoms became united against the common enemy. One dialect of the Romanzo developed itself, and took the name of the Galician, and afterwards became the language of the Portuguese, and remained their language when Portugal, in the twelfth century, formed a separate kingdom.

The Catalonian dialect flourished, and spread to the kingdom of Arragon, but was superseded by the Castilian dialect when Arragon and Castile were united under one sceptre. In the mountainous districts of Castile, there dwelt a hardy and valiant race, among whom the noble Spanish character was highly developed; and their language and ballad-poetry in time obtained a predominance over that of the neighboring kingdoms, until the Castilian came to be considered the standard Spanish of the united courts of Arragon and Castile, and was accepted as the language of the learned, while the others became dialects only of the common people.

Thus we see that the languages of Spain, like her ancient inhabitants, became blended and united, while the Moors and their language were finally expelled from the peninsula; but the Spanish language remained deeply imbued with the Oriental element, on account of the hundreds of years of neighborhood and intercourse — both in times of peace and war — with the Arabian Moors, who were a people of far more learning and culture than the original inhabitants whom they overcame, and who were subjected to Arabian influences for the better part of a thousand years. Having thus taken a glance at the condition of Spain and her inhabitants during the early and middle ages, and considered the influences which operated in forming the character of her people and language, we are the better prepared to appreciate the character and style of her ancient ballad-poetry, which flourished in Oriental glory during the time of the long and bloody struggles between the Christians and their Moorish invaders.

If we are to credit all that has been asserted concerning the antiquity of Spanish ballads, we may believe that there have been ballads in Spain from the most remote ages; for one writer upon the subject — and he a Spaniard — contended that Tubal, son of Japhet and grandson of Noah, arrived in Spain a hundred and forty years after the Deluge, and twenty-one hundred and sixty-three years before the birth of Christ, and gave the nations "a code of laws in couplets;" and Humboldt, travelling in the Basque provinces, collecting materials for his work on the aboriginal inhabitants, was shown some stanzas — which had been discovered in manuscript — of the time of Augustus, and still intelligible to the Basque highlanders.

But our purpose is only to take a hasty glance of Spanish ballad-poetry during the time that Spain was partly in possession of the Moors.

The early influences towards a more modern literature were given by the Provençal poets of the eleventh, twelfth, and thirteenth centuries, in the south of France and in Spain. They were sometimes called Romans, Troubadours, Trouvatori; and the Provençal language was called the Romana, Romanzo, Romance. It was derived in a great measure from the Latin, being, in fact, the corrupt Latin which was generally spoken by the inhabitants of the south of Europe after the over-throw of the Western Roman Empire; and it was the language in which the troubadour poets sang their fabliaux and romanzos, — those lays of chivalry, romance, and love.

The oldest of the troubadours, whose name and poems are known with certainty, was William, Count of Poitiers and Guienne (born A.D. 1071), though some poems of the same kind, and of an earlier date, are said to still exist: but these are earlier than any of the ballads now remaining in the English language; for, if we may believe the authority quoted by Bishop Percy, the oldest ballad now remaining in the English language is one called " Cuckow Song," beginning thus: —

> "Sumer is icumen in,
> Lhudè sing cuccu;
> Groweth sed[1] and bloweth med,[2]
> And spingeth[3] the wdè[4] nu."[5]

And this is no earlier than the time of Henry III., which was in the thirteenth century, being nearly contemporary with the oldest Scottish metrical romance known to exist, the celebrated lay of " Sir Tristrem," composed by

---

[1] Seed.   [2] Mead.   [3] Springeth.   [4] Wood.   [5] Anew.

Thomas of Erceldoune (the earliest Scottish minstrel), called Thomas the Rhymer, which metrical romance was preserved in manuscript for hundreds of years, and is now in the Advocates' Library at Edinburgh, Scotland, having been presented to the library by its possessor, Lord Auchinleck, some hundred and fifty years ago.

The oldest Spanish ballads are mostly on the subjects of love and war, recounting the adventures of knights and heroes, and the passions, pains, and delights of lovers. They differ very much from the early English and Scottish ballads both in spirit and tone, as well as in construction: for, while the English ballads are usually in iambic meter, the Spanish romanzo is generally trochaic, though some of it is really iambic; and a great peculiarity of Spanish versification is in the assonance, which the Spanish poets carried to the greatest perfection, sometimes, indeed, carrying it through entire lines, as not being satisfied with assonant rhymes alone. The stanzas are usually composed of four octo-syllabic lines: but a fifth and sixth line were added whenever it suited the poet's convenience, or to continue the story; and lines were added of six, of seven, or even of more syllables. Although the stanzas are usually of four octo-syllabic lines, still the second and fourth lines terminating in the same rhyme, or in an assonant rhyme, are frequently catalectic, having only three and a half trochaic feet, and terminating in an imperfect trochee; for the artless troubadours, or minstrel-poets, paid little attention to the correctness of quantity when weaving some well-known heroic story or tender tale of love into stanzas, which they sang to delighted and uncritical audiences, and usually with the accompaniment of the

"guiterne Moresche," or guitarra, — an instrument re-
sembling the cithera, or κιθαρα, of the ancients, — as their
Carthaginian or Egyptian ancestors had done thousands
of years before.[1]

As has already been said, there are extensive and rich
stores of ballads in the Spanish language, great numbers
of which originated during the long and bloody struggles
of the Christians against the Moors, and which recount
the chivalrous deeds of both Moors and Christians. While
many of these are truthfully historical, some of them are
evidently highly romantic; such, for example, as the
ballad of "The Moorish Calaynos," and the one of the
"Count Arnaldos," where "more is meant than greets
the ear." All of the stanzas in "Count Arnaldos" are
so truly poetical and sonorous, that the entire ballad will
be given here, even at the risk of spinning out this article to a wearisome length. It is as follows: —

"Who had ever such adventure,
    Holy priest or virgin nun,
As befell the Count Arnaldos
    At the rising of the sun?

"On his wrist the hawk was hooded;
    Forth with horn and hound went he,
When he saw a stately galley
    Sailing on the silent sea.

"Sail of satin, mast of cedar,
    Burnished poop of beaten gold, —
Many a morn you'll hood your falcon
    Ere you such a bark behold.

[1] Musical stringed instruments, very similar in form to the guitar,
were depicted upon Egyptian tombs of more than two thousand years
before the birth of Christ.

" Salls of satin, masts of cedar,
    Golden poops may come again,
But mortal ear no more shall listen
    To yon gray-haired sailor's strain.

" Heart may beat, and eye may glisten,
    Faith is strong, and Hope is free;
But mortal ear no more shall listen
    To the song that rules the sea.

" When the gray-haired sailor chanted,
    Every wind was hushed to sleep;
Like a virgin's bosom, panted
    All the wide-reposing deep.

" Bright in beauty rose the star-fish
    From her green cave down below,
Right above the eagle poised him, —
    Holy music charmed them so.

" ' Stately galley! glorious galley!
    God hath poured his grace on thee!
Thou alone mayst scorn the perils
    Of the dread devouring sea!

" ' False Almeria's reefs and shallows,
    Black Gibraltar's giant rocks,
Sound and sand-bank, gulf and whirlpool,
    All — my glorious galley mocks!

" ' For the sake of God, our maker!'
    (Count Arnaldos' cry was strong,)
' Old man, let me be partaker
    In the secret of thy song!'

> "'Count Arnaldos! Count Arnaldos!
> Hearts I read, and thoughts I know;
> Wouldst thou learn the ocean secret,
> In our galley thou must go.'"

That is poetry! poetry, indeed, wherein is shadowed forth some religious allegory; but Religion never yet called to her aid a sweeter muse.

Not less beautiful than the foregoing, although of an entirely different character, is the Moorish ballad, "The Bull-Fight of Gazul," wherein is described very minutely one of those bull-fights which were once the favorite amusement of the ancient inhabitants of the Spanish peninsula, in whose exciting dangers the Moors, after the conquest, learned to take as much delight as did the native Spaniards. The bull-fight here described seems to have been held in Granada, that last proud city that was held by the Moors in Spain; and by it we can see how surely an ancient ballad can preserve, and depict to future ages, the customs and manners of communities in ages long gone by. For want of space, only certain stanzas selected from this ballad can be given here. The Alcaydé Gazul, who is the hero of this ballad, was a Moorish knight of renown, who figures in the "Historia de las Guerras Civiles de Granada;" and the bravery and dexterity with which he meets and vanquishes the furious and enraged bulls, is repaid by the plaudits of the noble spectators, and the graceful smiles of his proud "ladye fayre," who bestows upon him first "the scarf whiter than the snow," and, afterwards, "the ring of price," from her own fair hand: —

"King Almanzor of Granada, he hath bid the trumpet
     sound;
He hath summoned all the Moorish lords from hills and
     plains around:
From Vega and Sierra, from Betis and Xenil,
They have come with helm and cuirass of gold and twisted
     steel.

"Eight Moorish lords of valor tried, with stalwart arm and
     true,
The onset of the beasts abide as they come rushing
     through:
The deeds they've done, the spoils they've won, fill all with
     hope and trust;
Yet, ere high in heaven appears the sun, they all have bit
     the dust!

"Then sounds the trumpet clearly, then clangs the loud
     tambour:
Make room, make room for Gazul! throw wide, throw wide
     the door!
Blow, blow the trumpet clearer still! more loudly strike
     the drum!
The Alcaydé of Algava to fight the bull doth come.

"And first before the king he passed, with reverence stoop-
     ing low,
And next he bowed him to the queen, and the infantas all
     a-row;
Then to his lady's grace he turned, and she to him did
     throw
A scarf, from out her balcony, was whiter than the snow.

"With the life-blood of slaughtered lords all slippery is the
  sand,
Yet proudly in the center now hath Gazul ta'en his stand;
And ladies look with heaving breast, and lords with anxious
  eye;
But firmly he extends his arm, — his look is calm and
  high.

"Three bulls against the knight are loosed, and two come
  roaring on;
He rises high in stirrup, forth stretching his *rejón;*
Each furious beast upon the breast he deals him such a
  blow,
He blindly totters, and gives back across the sand to go.

"'Turn, Gazul, turn!' the people cry. The third comes
  up behind;
Low to the sand his head holds he, his nostrils snuff the
  wind;
The mountaineers that lead the steers without stand whis-
  pering low,
'Now thinks this proud Alcaydé to stun Harpado[1] so!'

"Dark is his hide on either side; but the blood within doth
  boil,
And the dun hide glows as if on fire, as he paws to the
  turmoil;
His eyes are jet, and they are set in crystal rings of snow,
But now they stare with one red glare of brass upon the
  foe.

---

[1] The name of the bull.

"Now stops the drum; close, close they come; thrice meet,
 and thrice give back;
The white foam of Harpado lies on the charger's breast of
 black,
The white foam of the charger on Harpado's front of
 dun:
Once more advance upon his lance, — once more, thou fearless one!

"Once more, once more, in dust and gore to ruin must
 thou reel!
In vain, in vain, thou tearest now the sand with furious
 heel!
In vain, in vain, thou noble beast! I see, I see thee stagger:
Now keen and cold thy neck must hold the stern Alcaydé's
 dagger!

"They have slipped a noose around his feet, six horses are
 brought in,
And away they drag Harpado with a loud and joyful din:
Now stoop thee, lady, from thy stand, the ring of price
 bestow
Upon Gazul of Algava that hath laid Harpado low!"

As the last cadence of this spirit-stirring song rings
in the memory of the imaginative reader, so vivid, thrilling, and truly poetic are the descriptions, that, in imagination almost can there be heard an echo from those
plaudits of five hundred years agone; and the excited
eye of fancy will behold that brilliant audience of rich-
robed lords and "ladyes fayre;" and the excited mind
will be cognizant of the sudden hush and silence when

the loved one of Gazul "stoops from the stand" to bestow "the ring of price" upon her noble and proud Moorish cavalier.

I regret the want of space within the intended limits of this article to give additional specimens from the rich mines of Spanish ballad-poetry that lie open to the literary explorer.

Hundreds of them have been translated into the German and English, as well as into other languages: but, to be appreciated, they should be read and understood in their own peculiar and musical native Spanish rhymes; for, so read, they possess a charm that is lost even in the best of translations. But I cannot close even a hasty account of the early ballad-poetry of Spain, and leave a theme so deeply interesting, without some short comment upon the numerous ballads which relate to the times and history of the great and immortal Spanish hero, the world-renowned and ever-invincible Cid, Ruy Diaz de Bivar, called, by his own king, El Campeador, "the hero without an equal;" and, by the Moorish kings whom he vanquished, El mio Cid. The ballads that sing his fame are reckoned by the hundreds; for he, in conjunction with his noble and far-famed war-horse Babieca, has become the central figure of his time in all Spanish history, romance, and song. In him were concentrated all the elevated and noble qualities of the best age of chivalry, — an elevated valor that knew no fear, united with a noble generosity towards the weak or vanquished; a deep and unwavering loyalty to his king and country, joined to an unshaken fervor and devotion to his religion; a lofty and noble pride and self-reliance, wherein was mingled a deep and lasting scorn for every thing that

was dishonorable or base; and, blended with all the
noble qualities which made him the beau ideal of knight-
errantry, was an indomitable and childlike love of truth,
and a deep and unwavering love and devotion to the
fair, which made him, above all others, " a chevalier *sans
peur et sans reproche.*"

The great and immortal Cid Ruy Diaz, or — to give
him his name and cognomen in full — Don Rodrigo Diaz
de Bivar, el mio Cid, Campeador, was the flower of
Spanish chivalry, and the model of all the heroic virtues
of his age; and he has been celebrated in chronicle,
romance, and song, for the past eight hundred years.
He was born at Burgos, A.D. 1025 or 1026; for authori-
ties differ as to the precise year.

At the time of his birth the greater part of Spain was
in the possession of the Arabians, or Moors, who had
invaded it nearly four hundred years before; and, conquering city after city and province after province, had
driven the ancient inhabitants before them into the
northern and mountainous portions of the peninsula,
where they maintained several petty kingdoms or principalities.

The county of Castile — anciently called Burgos — became a separate kingdom in 1028; and Ferdinand I.
became its king, thereby founding the Castilian mon-
archy; and for him the great Cid conquered a part of
Portugal, and wrested many fair cities and provinces
from the Moors, which, by the valor of his arms, were
joined to the territories of his king; and, upheld and
borne onwards by his prowess, the ancient Gothic inhabitants, who had remained unconquered in the northern counties, made gradual and constant progress, and

reconquered many fair cities and provinces which had long been held by their Moslem invaders, to whom the name and person of the Cid became a lasting terror and a signal of sure defeat; for he soon gained the name of the invincible, and whomsoever he attacked he was sure to vanquish; for, as say or sing the ballads which recount his fame, he was a —

"Mighty victor never vanquished,
　　Bulwark of his native land;
Shield of Spain, her boast and glory,
　　Knight of the far-dreaded brand;
Venging scourge of Moors and traitors,
　　Mighty thunderbolt of war,
Mirror bright of chivalry,
　　Ruy el Cid, Campeador!"

The life and exploits of the Cid were in time made more familiar to the European world by the celebrated tragedy of the great Corneille, "Le Cid," which has held its place upon the classic stage of France for nearly three hundred years, and is familiar to all scholars who pretend to a knowledge of the French language the world over.

The Cid's father was Don Diego Lainez, a renowned warrior in his day, and descended from the great Lain Calvo, who represented one of the most ancient and noble families of Spain; and his mother was also nobly descended: so Rodrigo had the best and purest of Spanish blood in his veins.

While he was yet a youth, under twenty years of age, his father, who, through age and infirmities had become incapable of longer bearing arms, was grossly insulted

by the proud and domineering Count of Gormaz, who
went so far as to even give him a *soufflet*, or slap of
the hand upon the face; and that, too, in presence of the
king and court, — an indignity which, in the case of an
hidalgo of Spain, only blood could wash away, and over
which the Cid's father brooded so deeply after his return
from court to his own castle, that —

"Sleep was banished from his eyelids;
   Not a mouthful could he taste;
There he sat with downcast visage:
   Direly had he been disgraced.

"Never stirred he from his chamber;
   With no friends would he converse,
Lest the breath of his dishonor
   Should pollute them with its curse."

When Rodrigo learned the cause of his father's gloom,
his noble blood was fired by the disgrace which had been
cast upon his family; and, arming himself, he went forth
in search of the haughty offender, who was none other
than the father of Ximena Gomez, his own fair lady-
love; but, obeying the dictates of honor rather than
those of love, he sought out the offending lord, and addressed him in this wise: —

"How durst thou to smite my father?
   Craven caitiff! know that none
Unto him shall do dishonor
   While I live, save God alone.

"For this wrong I must have vengeance:
   Traitor, here I thee defy!
With thy blood alone my sire
   Can wash out his infamy!"

The haughty Count of Gormaz, laughing at the Cid's youth and inexperience, affected to despise his threats, whereupon Rodrigo told him that those who had noble escutcheons would never brook a wrong; and, calling upon him to defend himself, he set upon him so valiantly that the imperious count was soon overthrown and slain. Cutting off the head of his antagonist, he bore it to his own father, whom he addressed thus: —

> "Lay aside this grievous sorrow:
>   Lo! thine honor is secure;
> Vengeance hast thou now obtainèd,
>   From all stain of shame art pure.

> "Well have I avenged thee, father!
>   Well have sped me in the fight;
> For to him is vengeance certain
>   Who doth arm himself with right."

The father of Rodrigo, deeming his lost honor restored by the avenging arm of his brave son, thus addresses Rodrigo: —

> "At the chief place of my table,
>   Sit thee henceforth in my stead;
> He who such a head hath brought me,
>   Of my house shall be the head."

But Rodrigo, when he came to reflect upon what he had done, was himself plunged in gloom; for, although he had by his valor and prowess vindicated the honor of his house, and vanquished the haughty and renowned Don Gomez in fair fight, yet he felt, that, in so doing, he had taken the life of the father of his own fair and

well-beloved Ximena, who was dearer to him than all
the world beside; and how could he hope now to ever
possess her as his bride, with his own hands red with her
father's blood, although that blood had been shed in all
honor, and according to the code of the times which
governed the actions of all honorable men? And now,
although he despaired, for the time being, of possessing
her for his bride, yet he found himself utterly unable to
resign all hopes of eventually regaining her, and equally
unable to drive her fair image from his tortured mind;
for, in the language of one of the greatest of modern
bards, —

> "He who stems a stream with sand,
> And fetters flame with flaxen band,
> Has yet a harder task to prove,
> By firm resolve to conquer love!"

We shall see how Rodrigo sped him in such difficult
extremity. The ballads relate, that, when the fair Ximena
learned by whose hand her father had been "done to
death," she felt herself also in honor bound to take counsel of her head rather than of her heart; and so, in due
time, she presented herself before the good King Fer-
nando, clothed all in weeds of deepest mourning, and
followed by her train of maidens in similar array, to
claim vengeance upon him who had deprived her of a
father so deeply loved; and, falling upon her knees before
the king, she thus cried out for justice: —

> "Justice, king! I sue for justice,
> Vengeance on a traitorous knight.
> Grant it me! so shall thy children
> Thrive, and prove thy soul's delight.

"Like to God himself are monarchs
 Set to govern on the earth, —
All the vile and base to punish,
 And to guerdon virtuous worth.

"But the king who doth not justice
 Ne'er the scepter more should sway,
Ne'er should nobles pay him homage,
 Vassals ne'er his hests obey."

But the good king — since he was not able to restore
her father to life, and not wishing to punish or banish
so valorous and useful a knight as Rodrigo was beginning to show himself to be — puts off the fair Ximena,
most likely with many fair promises, never intended to
be fulfilled, trusting, like a wise monarch, to time and
circumstances to soften and change her mind; and, as
the sequel proved, he did not "lean upon a broken reed."

Nevertheless Ximena, impatient of delay, — feminine
trait, — returns again and again to urge her complaints
against Rodrigo, whom she still, however, dearly, though
secretly, loves; as the king, in truth, all along suspects.
Finally, on the occasion of one of those dolorous visits to
urge her suit against poor Rodrigo, she breaks out in this
wise: —

"King! six moons have passed away
 Since my sire was reft of life
By a youth whom thou dost cherish
 For such deeds of murderous strife.

"Four times have I cried thee justice;
 Four times have I sued in vain:
Promises I get in plenty;
 Justice, none can I obtain.

"Every day, at early morning,
　　To despite me more, I wist,
He who slew my sire doth ride by
　　With a falcon on his fist.

"At my tender doves he flies it;
　　Many of them hath it slain:
See! their blood hath dyed my garments
　　With full many a crimson stain."

The good king, seeing by this that Rodrigo was flying
his falcon at her doves, really with an eye to their mistress, hesitated no longer, but came at once pat to the
point, as the ballads relate, in this wise: —

"Say no more, O noble damsel!
　　Thy complaints would soften down
Bosoms were they hard as iron,
　　Melt them were they cold as stone.

"If I cherish Don Rodrigo,
　　For thy weal I keep the boy!
Soon, I trow, will this same gallant
　　Turn thy mourning into joy."

And so, in fact, it proved, to the great satisfaction of
all concerned; for the quarrel — like most love-quarrels,
when rightly managed by older heads, who know, of
course, just what is wanted — was easily made up: and
the happy pair were in due time united in those bonds
which give full liberty to quarrel in the future *ad libitum*
without the interference of king, commons, or neighbors.
And the lovers, made happy after long months of separa-
tion, met, and embraced each other tenderly: this was

before their marriage, mind you; and Rodrigo, gazing fondly upon his fair *fiancée*, thus addressed her: —

> "I did slay thy sire, Ximena,
> But, God wot, not traitorously;
> 'Twas in open fight I slew him:
> Sorely had he wrongèd me.

> "A man I slew, a man I give thee:
> Here I stand thy will to bide!
> Thou, in place of a dead father,
> Hast a husband by thy side."

And Ximena, like a sensible and good girl as she really was, blushed and smiled, and smiled and blushed; and thought, no doubt, as many a pretty maiden has thought since, that a young and valiant husband was far better, in her case, than an old father. And so the nuptials of the happy pair were celebrated with great pomp and rejoicing, the bishop himself tying the hymeneal knot, to make sure of its strength, and the king giving away the bride; and the streets through which they were to pass were strewed with sweet cypress, and the windows of the houses along their route were hung with cloth of gold; while the women showered wheat upon the bride as she passed along, in token of a wish that she might prove prolific; and, to adopt the language of a modern distich, slightly altered to make it fit the occasion, —

> "Minstrels sang, and music played,
> To think how happy she was made."

While, as to Rodrigo, the ballads of those times recount that —

"All approvèd well his prudence
And extollèd him with zeal:
Thus they celebrate the nuptials
Of Rodrigo of Castile."

But we must leave the song half sung, and the tale half told; for the purpose of this essay is, not to give a history of the Cid's life, but only to call the attention of the reader to the very many early Spanish ballads upon the subject, and at the same time give a few quotations from them to exemplify their literary value and poetic beauty; for it is well known that Dr. Southey has spoken of them in very disparaging terms. But we cannot help believing that he has unjustly undervalued their real worth and poetic beauty; for historical worth and real poetic beauty many of them certainly possess, as a large proportion of readers who take the pains to make their acquaintance will, without doubt, be convinced. Aside from the numerous ballads relating thereto, the life and adventures of the Cid also form the subject of one of the oldest, if not the oldest, long and continuous Castilian poem now extant, "Poema del Cid el Campeador;" but with that we are not at present concerned, as this essay has for its subject only ballad-poetry.

Although we are not writing the Cid's history, still it may not be uninteresting to the reader to be told that his life was long, and, for the most part, a prosperous one, though slanderous tongues often did him wrong; and those who were envious and jealous of his great valor and illustrious fame, often succeeded, for a time, in bringing upon him the disfavor of his king, so that he felt, at times, to the fullest extent, the truth of the great poet's dictum, that —

" He who ascends to mountain-tops shall find
   The loftiest peaks most wrapped in clouds and snow;
He who surpasses or subdues mankind
   Must look down on the hate of those below!''

But he never failed to re-appear in time with all his truth and valor and loyalty so resplendent as to burst through and dissipate all the dark clouds that calumny had been able to gather, for a time, around his name and fame; and in the end he could truthfully say, like royal Richard, —

"Now all the clouds that lowered upon our house
Are in the bosom of the ocean buried.''

The Cid spent the long years of his vigorous manhood and old age in almost continuous warfare against the Moslem invaders of Spain, and the enemies of his king; and one of his latest great achievements was the wresting of the rich and proud city of Valencia from the Moors, after a long and bloody siege of many months; and of Valencia he held possession till his dying day, although the Arabians, more than once, exerted themselves boldly to regain it. And at one time the great King of Tunis came to besiege it, landing on the Spanish shores with a numberless host of foot, and fifty thousand horse; but, nothing daunted, the Cid prepared to meet and repel them, saying, that "the greater the number of the enemy, the greater would be the spoils;'' and, taking Ximena and his two daughters to the top of the citadel, he pointed out to them with great delight the innumerable hosts of their invaders; and, as the ladies were alarmed at such a warlike array, he said, to cheer and comfort them, —

> "Fear thou not, my loved Ximena;
> Fear not ye, my daughters dear!
> While I live to wield Tizona,
> Ye, I wot, have naught to fear."

Tizona was the famous sword which he won in battle from a Moorish king years before. It was a blade so celebrated, and of such superior quality and worth, that he never failed to wield it himself in all his battles afterwards, and always with unfailing success. No wonder that the ladies were alarmed at the immensity of the host now arrayed against them; for the ballads say, that —

> "Toward the sea they cast their own eyes, —
> Foes did swarm along the coast;
> Round about the town they lookèd, —
> Everywhere a mighty host.

> "Tents were pitching, trenches digging,
> All to battle did prepare;
> Shouts of men, and war-steeds neighing,
> Drums and trumpets rent the air."

But the Cid, nothing daunted, prepared himself and his own invincible warriors to repel the invading hosts; for, says the ballad, —

> "But my good Cid, all perceiving,
> Rushèd on the enemy;
> 'Gainst their ranks he spurred Babieca,
> Shouting loud his battle-cry, —

" ' Aid us, God and Santiago!'
  Many a Paynim he laid low;
  To dispatch a foe he never
  Needed to repeat his blow.

" Well it pleased the Cid to find him
  Mounted on his steed once more,
  With his right arm to the elbow
  Crimsoned all with Moorish gore."

And so Valencia was relieved, the Moslems routed, and great were the spoils that were captured with their deserted camps. But we must pass over many interesting incidents in the Cid's life; such as the marriage of his daughters, and his noble vengeance upon their cowardly husbands, his own exile from court, the second marriage of his daughters, etc.; and refrain, for want of space, from quoting many a noble ballad relating thereunto, which it irks us very much to leave unsung, but which, from the necessity of making this notice brief, must be passed over in silence. Still, as we draw toward the close, and prepare to say adieu to a theme so loved, we linger still, and hesitate to lay aside the pen, as one who leaves the threshold that he loves, to wander far and long, will hesitate, and turn, and linger still to take one parting look of things most dear; so we — as some old ballad rises in the mind, to stir the blood by means of its deep pathos, or its chivalric memories of scenes and ages long gone by — still hesitate, and linger for a moment, and would fain prolong the pleasure which we ourselves have well experienced in studying these old songs, which Dr. Southey, in his unjust condemnation, has pronounced so worthless and so poor.

Again was the Cid besieged in his own fair city of
Valencia, — this time by a numerous host of Moslems,
headed by a King of Morocco; and it seems, by the tone
of the ballads relating to his later years, as if there was
a deep, rich strain of melancholy stealing over him
toward the close, to permanently pervade and sadden
that great soul, once so ardent and so martial. Still,
with some of his old-time bearing left, he sends back
this reply to the enemy, who demands the surrender of
his beloved Valencia: —

> "'Let your king prepare his battle;
>   I shall straightway order mine:
> Right dear hath Valencia cost me;
>   Think not I will it resign.

> "'Hard the strife and sore the slaughter;
>   But I won the victory,
> Thanks to God and to the valor
>   Of Castilian chivalry!'"

But, notwithstanding this bold reply, we can see that
his noble mind is sorely oppressed with unusual sadness;
for, while he is arming himself for the contest, he thus
addresses Ximena, who is aiding him in doing on his
warlike harness: —

> "'If, with deadly wounds in battle,
>   I this day my breath resign,
> To San Pedro de Cardeña
>   Bear me straight, Ximena mine.

> "'Wail me not, lest some base panic
>   On my chiefless warriors seize,
> But amid the call to battle
>   Make my funeral obsequies.

" 'This, my loved Tizon, whose gleamings
  Every foeman's heart appall;
Never let it lose its glory,
  Ne'er to hands of women fall.

" 'Should God will that Babieca
  Quit the strife alone this day,
And, without his lord returning,
  At thy gate aloud should neigh, —

" 'Open to him and caress him,
  Let him well be housed and fed;
He who well his master serveth
  Right well should be guerdonèd.

" 'Dear one, give me now thy blessing!
  Dry thine eyes, and cease to mourn!'
Then my Cid, he spurred to battle:
  Grant him, God, a safe return!' "

And he was again victorious, and returned in safety to
Ximena, notwithstanding all his gloomy forebodings, so
unusual heretofore, in all his warlike career. But, feeling
now that he was getting old and feeble, he knew that the
end could not be far away; and so, like a good soldier,
he made his preparations for the final conflict, and, calling his friends around him, he thus addressed them: —

" 'He who spareth no man living,
  Kings or nobles though they be,
At my door at length is knocking,
  And I hear him calling me.

" 'Friends, I sorrow not to leave you;
  If this life an exile be,
We who leave it do but journey
  Homeward to our family.' "

But, knowing that their enemies would take advantage of his death to regain Valencia, he gave these directions for the guidance of his friends, when his right arm would no longer be able to shield or succor them: —

> " 'Should the Moorish king assail you,
>   Call your hosts, and man the wall;
> Shout aloud, and let the trumpets
>   Sound a joyful battle-call.
>
> " 'Meantime then to quit this city
>   Let all secretly prepare,
> And make all your chattels ready
>   Back unto Castile to bear.
>
> " 'Saddle next my Babieca,
>   Arm him well as for the fight;
> On his back then bind my body,
>   In my well-known armor dight.
>
> " 'In my right hand tie Tizona;
>   Lead me forth unto the war;
> Bear my standard fast behind me,
>   As it was my wont of yore.
>
> " 'Then, Don Alvar, range thy warriors
>   To do battle with the foe;
> For right sure am I that on you
>   God will victory bestow.' "

And what the Cid foresaw soon arrived, for the Moors soon returned to besiege Valencia; but the Christians, in accordance with the Cid's instructions, had prepared for their own return to Castile, and in the dead of night they led forth Babieca; and, by the glare of many torches, they bound the dead body of the Cid firmly upright in the saddle, with the far-famed Tizona gleaming naked in his stiff right hand.

> "There he sat all stiff and upright,
>   So Gil Diaz did contrive;
> He who had not known the secret
>   Would have deemed him still alive.

> "By the fitful glare of torches
>   Forth they go at dead of night;
> Headed by their lifeless captain,
>   Forth they march unto the fight."

And then, by a miraculous interposition, good Santiago came to their aid; and the Moors saw what to them appeared to be an innumerable host, led on by a supernatural leader clothed in shining raiment; and, say the ballads, —

> "Seventy thousand Christian warriors,
>   All in snowy garments dight,
> Led by one of giant stature,
>   Mounted on a charger white.

> "On his breast a cross of crimson,
>   In his hand a sword of fire,
> With it hewed he down the Paynims,
>   As they fled, with slaughter dire."

And so they all turned away in dismay before the dead Cid and his miraculous allies; and thousands of them were borne down, and trampled to death in their headlong flight, while vast multitudes were drowned in their endeavors to get aboard their own ships.

And then the body of the Cid was borne back, amid mournings and lamentings, to his own native and dearly beloved Castile, where it was finally to repose, with the ashes of his ancestors, in the Convent of San Pedro de Cardeña, — a few miles to the east of Burgos, and not far from his own village of Bivar, — in a tomb which was honored by emperors and kings.

His faithful Ximena spent the remainder of her days in the same convent, near the dead body of her lord, keeping holy vigils by his tomb, whom she had so faithfully loved in life, and singing masses for the welfare of his soul; and she and their children were at last interred near him in San Pedro, while around and near them sleep the ashes of their ancestors, surrounded by those of kings, nobles, and other illustrious men.

Babieca, the noble war-horse that had borne our hero safely on his back through all his bloody battles, — now as celebrated as the Bucephalus of Alexander the Great, — was kindly cared for till his death; and no one was allowed to ever mount again upon that back which had so faithfully and nobly borne the Cid Rodrigo Diaz, "the honor of Castile and Spain."

" And neither Spain nor Araby could another charger bring
So good as he, or, certes, so worthy of a king;
But to behold him truly, and know him to the core,
You should have seen him bear the Cid when charging on
     the Moor."

He was buried deep beneath the trees in front of the convent where slept the ashes of his master; for the Cid had given directions in his will, that, "when ye bury Bavieca, dig deep; for shameful thing it were that he should be eaten by curs, who hath trampled down so much currish flesh of Moors." And above the entrance to the Convent of San Pedro is a mounted figure of the Cid, represented as in the act of striking down the Moors beneath the feet of the noble Babieca.

Thus we hope to have shown, by the few hasty quotations here given from the early ballads of Spain, and our imperfect historical remarks concerning them and the events which tended to call them forth, that these old songs, with their sweet undertone of sadness, which forms a strong element of their success and beauty, are worthy of a place in the heart and memory of all true lovers of the minstrel art. And had not the want of space, within the intended limits of this article, forbidden it, it would have been right pleasant to have given here, and at length, many another of those old ballads which breathe the chivalric spirit of that age when the warlike deeds of Spain's great hero inspired her unpretending minstrel-bards to perpetuate, for all time to come, the memory of those heroic deeds in sweet and spirit-stirring songs.

And it would be both pleasant and profitable to examine and recount some of those sad and pathetic ballads of a Moorish origin, which more particularly relate to that period and its events when the united forces of Arragon and Castile, under the successful direction of Ferdinand and Isabella, were finally working out the total ruin and downfall of the Moorish power in Spain; and forcing Boabdil, the last weak Moorish King of Granada, to cry out in bitterness of soul, —

"Farewell, farewell Granada! thou city without peer!"

And then it was that —

"There was crying in Granada when the sun was going
    down, —
Some calling on the Trinity, some calling on Mahoun!
Here passed away the Koran, there in the cross was borne,
And here was heard the Christian bell, and there the Moor-
    ish horn.

" 'Te Deum Laudamus!' was up the Alcala sung:
Down from the Alhambra's minarets were all the crescents
    flung;
The arms thereon of Arragon they with Castile's display;
One king comes in in triumph, one weeping goes away!"

Some of the ballads of this period are the beautiful
effusions which flowed from the richest of melancholy
fancies, wherein, in strains of deepest pathos, are poured
forth the very essence and abstract spirit of many griefs;
and, running through them all, there seems to be a con-
fluence of many sad thoughts, which were all awakened
by the same universal sources of national sorrow; and
all going. as it were, to make up one national reservoir
of pathetic and mournful feelings, embodied in strains
of deepest pathos, and tinged by the richest Oriental
fancy to mourn the loss and downfall of that " pride of
heathendom " and " bane of Christientie," the last and
best beloved stronghold of the Moors in Spain, — the rich
and noble kingdom of Granada.

HISTORICAL INTRODUCTION TO THE POEM OF KENILWORTH.

THE poem of Kenilworth was composed during a visit made by the author to the ruins of Kenilworth Castle in England. To those who have visited the ruins of Kenilworth, and read Scott's thrilling story of the same name, no word of explanation is necessary; but, to the many who have not yet enjoyed those exquisite pleasures, a word of historical explanation may not be amiss. The ruins of Kenilworth Castle are situated in the town of Kenilworth, county of Warwickshire, England, at about a hundred miles north-west from London. They are among the oldest and most extensive of the time-worn relics of the feudal ages. They date back with certainty to the times of Henry I., son of William the Conqueror, and, perhaps, much earlier. Henry I. granted the manor to his chamberlain, Geoffroi de Clinton, one of those Normans who settled in England after the Conquest. After the last of the de Clintons the castle was again vested in the Crown, as it was many times afterwards in the ages that followed; and for many ages Kenilworth was a place of the first importance, and fills an important place in history. Often vested in the Crown, it was likewise often possessed by some of the greatest of England's nobles, such as the de Montforts, the Bolingbrokes, and the renowned John of Gaunt, — "time-honored Lan-

caster," — who had here his favorite residence. Henry
VIII. bestowed much cost in repairing and enlarging the
castle. And Queen Elizabeth bestowed the castle and
manor upon Robert Dudley (son of the Duke of North-
umberland), whom she created Earl of Leicester, and
whom, it has been said, she would willingly have married. In July, 1575, took place the "virgin queen's"
celebrated visit to her beloved Leicester in his castle of
Kenilworth, when and where were held those world-
renowned *fêtes* and tournaments of which Scott has given
us such an enchanting description. And, indeed, to the
pilgrim and poet the ruins of Kenilworth, grand and
beautiful in decay, owe their chief charms to the spells
of enchantment and potent attraction that have been
thrown around them by the pen of the Scottish novelist;
and a thousand pleasant but saddening memories will
rise up in the pilgrim's mind while wandering among
these stately and extensive ruins, and his heart will often
throb with sorrow and sympathy for the woes and unre-
quited love of poor Amy Robsart. Although Kenilworth
is now in ruins, yet is it grand and noble even in decay,
and stands to-day, and long will stand, a proud witness
of the pride and splendor of the feudal ages. Occupying
acres of ground, it is composed of almost innumerable
lofty towers and long lines of connecting buildings, ex-
tending around and nearly inclosing an extensive court,
or tilt-yard, with vast piles of lofty buildings projecting
at irregular intervals of its circuit; for almost every one
of its noble possessors made, in turn, some extensive alter-
ations or additions. The Earl of Leicester alone is said
to have expended in his time about sixty thousand pounds
of English money in additions and repairs, — a sum equal

in value to more than a million of dollars of our present money. The great banqueting hall, adjoining Mervyn's tower, was built by John of Gaunt, — a most noble apartment, nearly a hundred feet in length, and half as wide, and of great height. Its floor was supported on a stone vaulting, resting on parallel rows of massive pillars; and its windows were of great height, filled with tracery, and transomed, with the spaces between them paneled; while they, and the fireplaces on each side, were richly ornamented. It also contained two grand oriel windows, — one looking east into the great court, and one looking west into the chase. But Kenilworth has now lain for ages dismantled and in ruins, and reft of all its ancient glory; but in its day it was a most princely abode. Aside from its banqueting halls and state apartments, it contained rooms for more than a hundred beds, to accommodate its princely possessors and their retinues. Kenilworth's final ruin was completed during the civil wars that followed the overthrow of Charles I.; and, from being a stately and princely palace, it became a vast and dismantled ruin, now all overgrown with aged ivy-branches, which seek to shield its crumbling walls and towers from the beating storms and moaning winds which batter and wear its decaying battlements, and moan through its deserted and ruined halls. After the restoration, the ruined castle and lands of Kenilworth were granted to a son of Chancellor Hyde; and, by the marriage of one of his female descendants, they passed to Thomas Villiers, Baron Hyde, afterwards created Earl of Clarendon, whose descendants are the present possessors. A few years ago large portions of the ruins showed signs of falling, and Earl Clarendon caused them to be strengthened, and partially restored the great hall, and repaired some of the external walls, as well as some parts called Leicester's buildings. In so doing, the workmen discovered underground apartments, cells, and passages which had lain concealed and unknown for ages. And thus to-day stands ruined Kenilworth, — grand and stately, even in decay, with some of its slowly crumbling towers still rising to a height of more than seventy feet, to attest the grandeur and importance of princely Kenilworth in those far-off days when poor Amy Robsart, whose glowing beauty would well have graced its princely halls, was wiping her tear-stained eyes, a close prisoner, beneath one of these lofty towers whose mistress it was her right to be; while Leicester, who should have protected her in that right, was basely paying court to royalty in the person of his sovereign queen.

" And good Queen Bess was lodged within these towers,
Where now the ivy trails, and ruin darkly lowers."

KENILWORTH.

"Full many a traveler oft hath sighed,
    And, pensive, wept the countess' fall,
As, wandering onwards, they've espied
    The haunted towers of Cumnor Hall.

"Now naught was heard beneath the skies:
    The sounds of busy life were still,
Save an unhappy lady's sighs
    That issued from that lonely pile."
                 Cumnor Hall,[1] by MICKLE.

I.

O KENILWORTH! thy crumbling walls
    Speak sadly of the past to me;
Now standing in thy ruined halls,
    Thy mighty past I well can see.

II.

I well can see the courtly throng
    That peopled once thy lordly walls;
Gay knights and dames, who trooped along,
    And woke to mirth thy princely halls.

[1] See Appendix at the end of the poem.

III.

Thy lordly towers that proudly reared
　　Their lofty heads to prop the sky :
What though those towers have disappeared?
　　Though walls are rent, and moat is dry?

IV.

What though to-day no banners float
　　Proudly o'er thy embattled walls?
What though no waters fill thy moat,
　　No drawbridge rises now or falls?

V.

What though no warder on thy walls
　　Paces to-day his stately round?
What though no echoing bugle-calls
　　Through keep and court and tower resound?

VI.

What though no guards or seneschals,
　　With hurrying footsteps to and fro, —
Roused by the echoing bugle-calls, —
　　Prepare to meet if friend or foe?

VII.

What though thy glories all are past?
　　Thou once wert mighty, world-renowned,
Though now the moaning autumn blast
　　Seems thy sad requiem to sound.

VIII.

And rent and ruin everywhere
    Fill the beholder's mind with woe,
Though mantling ivy's shielding care
    Less ghastly lets thy ruins show.

IX.

Here desolation reigns supreme,
    And crumbling ruins strew the ground ;
Here, where such earthly pomp was seen,
    Ruin and silence most abound !

X.

N'importe ! By aid of Fancy's eye,
    I gaze adown the vanished years,
And all thy pomp and panoply
    To my rapt vision now appears.

XI.

As by some great enchanter's power,
    The vanished years are backward rolled,
Till keep and court and lordly tower,
    Again all perfect, I behold !

XII.

Again the warders mount the walls,
    And princely banners flout the sky ;
And England's beauties throng thy halls,
    Guarded by England's chivalry.

XIII.

I see the virgin queen again
　　Enthroned in thy high princely hall, —
A "virgin queen," at least in name,
　　Beloved by some, and feared by all.

XIV.

And graceful Leicester, bowing low,
　　Pays homage on his bended knee,
And courts his sovereign with a show
　　Of mingled love and loyalty.

XV.

While England's nobles, standing by,
　　Look smilingly his suit upon,
Deeming he mounts to royalty,
　　His sovereign's heart already won.

XVI.

Little that sovereign deems that here,
　　Within these walls, a lovelier one
Is pouring now the silent tear,
　　To whom thy plighted faith is sworn.[1]

[1] During Queen Elizabeth's celebrated visit to Kenilworth, and while the Earl of Leicester was entertaining her with such splendor, and also paying her such marked attention that he was generally considered as her favored and accepted lover, the beautiful but unhappy Amy, to whom he had been secretly married, was confined a close prisoner in a tower of the castle called Mervyn's Bower; and it was only after her escape from her prison, and while she was trying to fly, — she knew not

XVII.

Wily deceiver! dread the hour
　　When all the falsehoods of thy heart
Are bared to her offended power,
　　Lest thy poor head and body part.

XVIII.

She is the daughter of a sire
　　Who ne'er brooked injury or slight;
Her soul is filled with Henry's fire:
　　Oh, dread the force of her roused might!

XIX.

The wounded lion, when at bay,
　　Is meek compared to her wild rage
When jealousy her heart shall sway,
　　And vengeance shall her thoughts engage.

whither,—that she was accidentally seen by the queen. And only those who are well acquainted with the character of Elizabeth, and have read Scott's thrilling description of the scene, can imagine or comprehend the terrible force of the queen's rage as she gave way to her roused jealousy and wounded pride; and the explosion of her anger bowed the haughty Leicester to the earth, and shook him like an aspen leaf. "' And will he be the better for thy intercession?' said the queen, leaving Tressilian, and rushing to Leicester, who continued kneeling; 'the better for thy intercession, thou doubly false, thou doubly foresworn?—of thy intercession, whose villany hath made me ridiculous to my subjects, and odious to myself? I could tear out mine eyes for their blindness!'"

XX.

But not for Leicester, nor for queen,
  Do weary pilgrims, year by year,
Seek out this sad and solemn scene
  To muse in mournful silence here.

XXI.

Ah, no! nor that these ruined walls
  Once owned de Montfort as their lord,
Or echoed to wild battle-calls
  Beneath Plantagenet's own sword.

XXII.

Oh, no! nor that great John of Gaunt —
  "Time-honored Lancaster" — dwelt here.[1]
Not for such names do pilgrims haunt
  These scenes, and o'er them drop the tear.

---

[1] Henry, Earl of Derby and Duke of Lancaster, died in peaceful possession of Kenilworth in the thirty-fifth of Edward III., leaving two daughters as his joint heiresses, — Maud, aged twenty-two, and Blanch, nineteen. Maud afterwards married William, Duke of Bavaria; and Blanch brought Kenilworth as her portion of the inheritance, in marriage, to one of its most illustrious possessors, — John of Gaunt, son of Edward III.; and the king soon after created him Duke of Lancaster, — the "time-honored Lancaster" of Shakspeare. Kenilworth Castle became to him a favorite place of abode, and he added largely to it; and some portions of the ruins still bear his name, and show the magnificence of his tastes.

XXIII.

A deeper charm than all combined
　Is woven round these crumbling stones, —
The spells of a great master mind
　Mingled with injured Beauty's moans.

XXIV.

When the pale moon in virgin blaze
　Silvers each crumbling tower and wall,
And pours a flood of silvery rays
　Through the old grand baronial hall;

XXV.

Then moving shadows come and go
　Through ivy-branches rent and torn,
Which, to the roused-up fancy, show
　Like flitting maiden's half-seen form.

XXVI.

And sighing night winds, moaning round
　Through broken arch and crumbling tower,
Startle the ear, like distant sound
　Of maiden's moans in prison-bower.

XXVII.

And softened echoes from the dell,
　Like wavelets on the silver sands,
Fall on the ear like distant knell
　Of death-bell rung by spirit-hands!

XXVIII.

Then will the pilgrim's throbbing heart
　The soul's deep sympathy disclose,
And in the poet's eye will start
　A tear for Amy Robsart's woes.

XXIX.

And poet's head and poet's soul
　Will bow in reverence deep and long
To him who could all hearts control, —
　To Scotland's bard, her king of song!

XXX.

To Scotland's bard, whose mighty mind
　Wove magic spells these ruins round,
Where woman's love and woes combined
　Make this forever holy ground!

APPENDIX TO THE POEM OF "KENILWORTH."

ALTHOUGH Sir Walter Scott, in his grand romance of "Kenilworth," has represented some of the most deeply interesting scenes in that touching story as passing in Kenilworth Castle, yet the entire tragedy of the murder of the *real* Countess of Leicester took place at Cumnor Hall, near Oxford, many miles distant from Kenilworth Castle. And it was the beautiful old ballad of "Cumnor Hall," on the tragic death of the real Countess of Leicester, by William Julius Mickle, a Scottish poet of the eighteenth century, that first suggested to Sir Walter the idea of his noble story. The true history of the tragic death of the *real* Countess of Leicester is to be found in Ashmole's "Antiquities of Berkshire;" and the entire tragedy took place in Cumnor Hall.

Three or four miles from Oxford — the seat of the great English university — are the ruins of Godstow Abbey; but very little is now left of Godstow, and only a few standing walls were to be seen when the writer of this took pains to visit the place a few years ago; and those sacred remains were then used as a cow-pen: —

"To what base uses we may return, Horatio!"

But in the neighborhood of ruined Godstow were the broad lands of the ancient manor of Cumnor Hall, once belonging to the monks of Abington.

At the suppression of the monasteries by Henry VIII. in the sixteenth century, the said manor of Cumnor was conveyed to one —— Owen, the possessor of Godstow at the time; and, according to Ashmole's "Antiquities," there was in the said house of Cumnor Hall a chamber called Dudley's chamber, where the Earl of Leicester's wife was murdered, of which murder, according to Ashmole, the following is, in part, the true story: —

"Robert Dudley, Earl of Leicester, a very goodly personage, and singularly well featured, being a great favorite to Queen Elizabeth, it was thought, and commonly reported, that had he been a batchelor or widower the queen would have made him her husband; to this end, to free himself of all obstacles, he commands, or perhaps with fair flattering intreaties, desires his wife, the Countess of Leicester, to repose herself here at his servant Anthony Forster's house, who then lived in the aforesaid manor-house (i.e., in Cumnor Hall), and also prescribed to Sir Richard Varney (a prompter to this design), at his coming hither, that he should first attempt to poison her, and, if that did not take effect, then by any other way whatsoever to dispatch her.

"This, it seems, was proved by the report of Dr. Walter Bayly, sometime fellow of New College, then living in Oxford, and professor of physic in that university, whom, because he would not consent to take away her life by poison, the earl endeavored to displace him the court. This man, it seems, reported for most certain, that there was a practice in Cumnor among the conspirators to have poisoned this poor innocent lady a little before she was killed, which was attempted after this manner: —

" They, seeing the good lady sad and heavy (as one
that well knew by her other handling, that her death was
not far off), began to persuade her that her present dis-
ease was abundance of melancholy and other humours,
&c., and therefore would needs counsel her to take some potion, which she absolutely refusing to do, as still suspect-
ing the worst, whereupon they sent a messenger on a day
(unawares to her) for Dr. Bayly, and entreated him to
persuade her to take some little potion by his direction,
and they would fetch the same at Oxford, meaning to
have added something of their own for her comfort, as
the doctor upon just cause and consideration did suspect,
seeing their great importunity, and the small need the
lady had of physic, and therefore he peremptorily denied
their request, misdoubting (as he afterwards reported),
lest, if they had poisoned her under the name of his
potion, he might have been hanged for a colour of their
sin ; and the doctor remained still well assured that this
way taking no effect, she would not long escape their
violence, which afterwards happened thus : —

" For Sir Richard Varney above-said (the chief pro-
jector in this design), who, by the earl's order, remained
that day of her death alone with her, with one man only
and Forster, who had that day forcibly sent away all her
servants from her to Abington market, about three miles
distant from this place. They (I say, whether first stifling
her, or else strangling her) afterwards flung her down a
pair of stairs and broke her neck, using much violence
upon her ; but, however, though it was vulgarly reported
that she by chance fell down stairs (but still without hurt-
ing her hood that was upon her head), yet the inhabitants
will tell you there that she was conveyed from her usual

chamber where she lay, to another where the bed's head
of the chamber stood close to a privy postern door, where
they in the night came and stifled her in her bed, bruised
her head very much, broke her neck, and at length flung
her down stairs; thereby believing the world would have
thought it a mischance, and so have blinded their vil-
lainy."

Such (in part) is the true story of the murder of the
real Countess of Leicester; and Scott, in the preface to
his grand romance of "Kenilworth," tells us that he
"borrowed several incidents, as well as names, from
Ashmole's ' Antiquities; ' but that his *first* acquaintance
with the history [of the murder of the real Countess of
Leicester] was through the pleasing medium of verse,"
alluding, thereby, to the fine old ballad of "Cumnor
Hall," by Mickle, two stanzas of which I have placed at
the head of my poem of " Kenilworth " as a motto.

G. D.

1882.

THE WIZARD'S GRAVE.

"Each varying shade of many colored life he drew,
Exhausted worlds, and then created new."

I.

I stood by Avon's winding stream ;
   And tearful eyes were gazing on
A tomb where sleep, in endless dream,
   The ashes of proud " Stratford's Swan. " [1]
And mortal heads were bending low
   In reverence round that humble tomb,
Where, flitting ever to and fro,
   Strange throngs of shadowy forms find room.

II.

With Fancy's eye I see them all, —
   A wondrous, shadowy spirit-throng !
With ashy lips some seem to call,
   And some seem chanting airy song ;

[1] In an unpretending church in the rural town of Stratford, and near the sweetly gliding River Avon, sleeps, beneath a plain and humble slab, all that was mortal of the great and immortal Shakspeare, "the sweet Swan of Avon," but infinitely greater in his humble grave than all the kings who lie in gorgeous tombs in Westminster Abbey.

Mouthing and moping here and there,
　　Some glide, all ghostlike, to and fro;
While some seem spirits of the air
　　Watching the ways of those below.

III.

Many with coronets are crowned,
　　Some robed like haughty kings and queens;
And one, with gaze bent on the ground,
　　In weeds of woe. a mourner seems:
In "inky cloak." [1] his ashen face
　　E'er thrills me with its solemn stare,
While ever by him seems to pace
　　A kingly, ghostlike form of air.

IV.

Which seeing, he, with wonder thrilled
　　And outstretched hands, on bended knee.
In supplicating mood. seems filled
　　With doubt and dread uncertainty:
Thus gazing on that kingly form,
　　He seems to list some dreadful tale;
For, like the rack of driving storm,
　　Dark shades flit o'er his features pale.

---

[1] "*Hamlet.* 'Tis not alone my *inky cloak*, good mother,
　　Nor customary suits of solemn black,
　　No, nor the fruitful river in the eye,
　　Together with all forms, modes, shows of grief,
　　That can denote me truly: these, indeed, seem,
　　For they are actions that a man might play:
　　But I have that within which passeth show;
　　These but the trappings and the suits of woe."
　　　　　　　　　　　　Hamlet, Act 1. Scene 2.

V.

It thrills the soul to see the throngs
  Of airy forms that there find room ;
While Fancy's ear hears airy songs
  Sighed out above that wizard's tomb,
And Fancy's eye beholds with fear
  Such sights as would appall the brave, —
The murderer's knife, the victim's tear,
  Woman's remorse, and maiden's grave.

VI.

And one dark form, appalled with fears
  From meditation deep, profound,
With sudden " flaws and starts," appears
  To chase an " air-drawn dagger " [1] round !
And near him a right queenly form
  Her pallid hands appears to lave ;
And of " damned spots," of murder born,
  In walking sleep, she seems to rave. [2]

---

[1] " *Lady Macbeth.* This is the very painting of your fear :
This is the *air-drawn dagger*, which, you said,
Led you to Duncan. Oh, these *flaws and starts*
(Impostors to true fear) would well become
A woman's story at a winter's fire,
Authorized by her grandam."   *Macbeth*, Act iii. Scene 4.

[2] " *Waiting-woman.* Lo you, here she comes ! This is her very guise ;
and, upon my life, fast asleep. Observe her.

Doctor. What is it she does now ? Look how she rubs her hands.

Waiting-woman. It is an accustomed action with her to seem thus
washing her hands : I have known her continue in this a quarter of an
hour.

Lady Macbeth (walking in her sleep and rubbing her hands). Yet
here's a spot. Out, *damned spot !* out, I say ! — One, two : why, then
'tis time to do't."   *Macbeth*, Act v. Scene 1.

VII.

While weird and withered forms around
   In magic circles seem to turn,
Where, rising ghostlike from the ground,
   Blue, lurid flames round caldron burn : [1]
As if by magic, mingle all
   These beings of a wizard's brain ;
While airy voices seem to call,
   They pass, and turn, and come again.

VIII.

Why turn they here in endless round?
   Why hover ever o'er this tomb,
Obeying, as by magic bound,
   His ashes in their final home?
Great wizard of the world, sleep on !
   The world, in reverence, bows to thee ;
Millions of ages yet to come
   To thy great name shall bend the knee !

IX.

Reader, go stand beside that grave !
   The sights I saw shall meet your view :
If not, then pray your soul to save :
   That wizard's charms are not for you ;

---

[1] " *Witches.*   Round about the caldron go;
     In the poisoned entrails throw. —
     Double, double toil and trouble;
     Fire, burn; and, caldron, bubble."
               Macbeth, Act iv. Scene 1.

For there for ever must that throng
   Of shadowy beings wheel their round,
And airy voices breathe wild song,
   Where the great wizard's grave is found.

TO EDWIN BOOTH AS HAMLET.

The following tribute to Edwin Booth, in his great and unrivalled character of Hamlet, was composed in honor of his appearance in that character at the Park Theatre, in Boston, in March, 1880, after an absence of some years. It was published in "The Boston Daily Evening Traveller," and from that paper copied into others, while Mr. Booth, as Hamlet, was nightly crowding the theatre to its utmost capacity with the most fashionable and delighted audiences.

Hail! hail! all hail! thy glad return!
For now the classic lamp shall burn
Once more to light our modern stage,
Undimmed by follies of the age;
And we with joy shall hear again
Great Shakspeare's deep impassioned strain,
Interpreted with grace refined
By thine own lofty, classic mind.

Too long our stage hath cumbered been
By follies of a lighter mien,
Where show and jest of simple mood
Are served for intellectual food:
Shame on the age that thus demands
Such nourishment from actors' hands!

Full well we know the stage hath been
In every age the mimic scene
Where the true temper of the age
Repeats itself upon the stage.
In the great days of Greece and Rome,
The noblest actions there were shown ;
Yet, long before their overthrow,
Their stage, like ours, held empty show :
Effeminacy wrought decay
Of strength that held the world at bay.
Not all the powers of foreign foe
Could lay their power and grandeur low,
Till love of wealth and show at length
Had sapped their stern and manly strength.

And can we hope to 'scape the doom
That gave to Greece and Rome a tomb?
And doth not now our modern stage,
Like theirs, the same dark fate presage?
The stage, with truth, as Shakspeare told,
Doth " mirror up to nature hold ; "
And there " the body of the times "
" In form and pressure" truly shines.

We hail thee with a joyous heart,
And long to see thee play thy part :
Let Stratford's Swan exalt his crest,
And soar in grandeur o'er the rest !

Put modern follies all to rout :
Oblivion's wave shall wash them out ;
But ne'er for wealth or present fame,
Mingle with them thy noble name,
That name which long, within the mind,
Hath been with Shakspeare's intertwined,
Till unto us, as to our sires,
It lights the glow of classic fires.
Descend thou, not from Shakspeare's line,
To follies of the present time,
But hold untiringly thy course,
Like tried and trusted battle-horse.
Heed envy not ! be of good cheer,
Nor falter in thy high career !
For ne'er did towering genius soar,
But raised the envy of the boor ;
And proof most sure of lofty state,
When marked by envy and by hate.
But heed it not, and coming time
Thy name with laurel wreath shall twine.

Thousands and thousands everywhere
Now watch thee in thy great career :
Oh, fail us not ! our faith in thee
Is firm as human faith can be, —
Firm as the adamantine rock
That meets unmoved the ocean's shock.
Where northern tempests roar and rave ;
Where bursts the northern ocean's wave :

Yet strength and grandeur, there combined,
Meet and hurl back both wave and wind:
So let thine own proud soul stand firm,
And hate and envy meet with scorn;
For godlike is the thirst of fame,
And the desire for deathless name:
And ages yet unborn shall hear
The story of thy proud career.

As old men's memories yet are stirred
By thy sire's name as Richard Third,
So shall thine own, in coming time,
With that of Hamlet ever shine!
And name of Hamlet, shall, in sooth,
Bring to the mind the name of Booth!
And millions yet unborn shall say
How Booth did Hamlet's woes portray;
How thus, and thus, he played the part;
How fired the soul, how thrilled the heart.

Is there no art by which are caught
The airy lines of changing thought?
No heaven-born art, to catch and trace
The doubt and wonder in thy face?
When there, upon thy bended knee,
A father's ghost thou first dost see?

And when, in sweet Ophelia's heart,
No longer sure of lover's part,

What tender sorrow — grief refined —
In thy distracted, doubting mind!
And poor Ophelia, doubting too
What rightfully to think or do,
Bewails thy reason overthrown, —
" Like sweet bells jangled out of tune! "
Her heart, her hopes, now tempest-tossed,
She fades and dies, — her reason lost!
Yet, like the swan, she singing dies,
Twining sweet flowers with memories ;
Her fading sighs, her dying moans,
As tender as the wind-harp's tones.

And when thy mother thou dost chide,
While yet she seeks her guilt to hide, —
Oh God! is there no art can trace
The agony upon thy face?
Can trace and give, to coming time,
To see that agony sublime?

And when at last a father's death
Is well avenged, and thy last breath
Is drawn in agony and pain,
Lest coming time thy action blame, —
Oh, then! the living thoughts that trace
Their lines upon thy dying face!

Of all the cunning hands that weave
The lines to make cold marble breathe, —

Of all those hands, oh! are there none
Can chisel out a dying groan?
Press on! press on!   Oh, never fear,
Nor falter in thy grand career!
Though art may fail, a deathless name
Awaits thee with the crown of fame!

TRIBUTE TO OLIVER WENDELL HOLMES.

ON HIS SEVENTIETH BIRTHDAY.

When the poet Oliver Wendell Holmes reached the age of seventy years, the publishers of "The Atlantic Monthly"—to which, Dr. Holmes had long been a constant contributor—gave a reception and breakfast to the veteran poet in honor of the occasion, and many poems were written in celebration of the event; and, among others, the following was written in honor of that occasion, and afterwards published in "The Daily Evening Traveller."

"How shall an old man keep young?
  Seek the spell all tribes among
  In the lore of every tongue;
  Seek it in the catacombs
  Buried in Egyptian tombs;
  Lastly search in Florida
  For the fount which Leon saw."

J. F. C. *to* O. W. H.

Why seek dark spells strange tribes among,
Or mystic lore in foreign tongue?
Why search through the dark catacombs,
Or in old Egypt's mouldy tombs?
Why seek for magic's mystery
To guard against what ne'er can be?
What need of charm or spell, in sooth,
Or of the fabled Fount of Youth?

132

For be it said with accent bold,
Holmes never was nor can be old;
His own sweet songs, of love and truth,
Are his unfailing Fount of Youth.

Whoever heard it said or sung
That Homer, Virgil, were not young?
Whoever heard it sung or told
That Burns or Byron e'er grew old?
And know you not that lofty mind
Was ne'er by nature's laws confined?
Mind pierces laws of nature through:
No need that I tell this to you.

Holmes bears in his own loving heart
The magic and the mystic art,
The glamour and the charm untold,
By which he never can seem old;
He pours from his own dulcet tongue
The magic words that keep him young;
And heart and brain the charm combine
Which make him your friend — and mine.
Yes, mine he is, although, 'tis true,
We ne'er had earthly interview:
The Fates to me that joy ne'er gave —
Perchance ne'er will — this side the grave;
And to me it may ne'er be given
To clasp his hand this side of heaven.

N'importe! I revel in his song.
And my heart bears his love along;
Like you, I prize his mirth and wit,
And oft they give me laughing " fit."
I con them o'er and o'er again,
Till every button feels the strain;
And in my heart I bless the man
Who " ne'er writes funny as he can."

His songs cheer me on life's rough road :
They ease my heart of weary load,
And bring to me the same sweet spell,
As if, like you, I knew him well;
My soul warms with poetic fire,
Like yours, whene'er he tunes his lyre;
And, when he strikes a sadder strain,
We both resist its power in vain;
For, be his strain or sad or free,
He charms each heart to sympathy.

His sweet songs bear no marks of age;
Freshness and youth embalm each page;
In every flowing line we see
The fairest flowers of minstrelsy,
Untouched by any breath of cold :
Then how can he be growing old?

Away with such unwelcome word,
And let it never more be heard !

But hail him now, and hail him long,
Our dear New England's prince of song !
Oh, may his lyre ne'er lose a string,
Nor chilling age around it cling
To muffle its sweet voice of song !
Which heaven grant may cheer us long,
May cheer us through life's pilgrimage,
And millions more from age to age !

Then let us love him while we may,
And prize him more from day to day :
His heart for all bears love untold,
And never, never can grow old.

But, oh ! should envious Death appear,
And bear him to some higher sphere, —
We would not say that he was dead,
But to the starry heavens fled,
Where golden lyres for ever sound,
Where songs of love and truth resound ;
There his great soul and tuneful lyre
Shall bear their part in heavenly choir ;
Then may our souls be borne afar
To meet him on that better star.

OLIVER AND JAMES.

(First published in " The Daily Evening Traveller.")

The seventieth birthday of the Rev. James Freeman Clarke was honored by a public celebration of the event in the Church of the Disciples; and Oliver Wendell Holmes — in honor of whose seventieth birthday Dr. Clarke had written a poem a few months before — wrote, in turn, a very touching poem to his college classmate and life-long friend, in which occurs this stanza : —

> " How few still breathe this mortal air
> We called by schoolboy names!
> You still, whatever robe you wear,
> To me are only James!"

AGAIN we hear the solemn chime,
Pealed by the iron tongue of Time ;
The solemn chime — " His seventieth year " —
Again breaks on the startled ear,
As if the world had all grown old,
And Youth was dead, and Hope was cold,
And gray-haired Time, without a fear,
Could sound for all a seventieth year,
As if the race of living men
Had donned at once " threescore and ten."

It seems to me but yesterday
That James awoke his tender lay,

136

Where Friendship sang, in sweetest strains,
For Oliver, the love of James.

It filled the eye with Pity's tears
When Oliver saw seventy years;
And James, to celebrate the day,
Awoke for him that tender lay
Where friendship tried, with artful strain,
To soothe for Oliver the pain, —
The pain — regret — perchance the tears,
That wrapped him with those seventy years.
Now James, in turn, has reached the age
Allotted to life's pilgrimage, —
The numbered years, " threescore and ten,"
The Psalmist counts for mortal men ;
And Oliver, in tender strains,
Sings back, in turn, to comfort James,
And strives with all a minstrel's art
To cheer dear James and soothe his heart ;
And wreathes his brow and wipes his tears,
Till he forgets his seventy years.

And thus, like brothers tried and true,
They nobly march life's journey through ;
And hand in hand the bard and sage
Are winding down life's pilgrimage ;
And as they go, to cheer the road
And ease the heart of weary load,

With tender songs and noble speech,
Each one, in turn, doth comfort each:
With many a look to that dear time
When both, in youth, began to climb, —
To climb the shining heights of Fame,
Where both have won a noble name, —
The heights of Fame, where now they stand
The noblest in their native land.
Oh, may their days be lengthened long,
To cheer with counsel and with song!

And shall my harp be silent now,
When seventy years wreathe James's brow?
My harp that woke its feeble lays
To sound for Oliver meet praise, —
Meet praise for him when seventy years
Had wrapped him in their weighty cares?

If to that harp one chord remains,
Now let it sound, in turn, for James!
By noble sage and noble bard
Now let its dying notes be shared!
And when for them its dying strain
Shall cease, it ne'er may sound again.

Well, let it break: no eye shall weep,
Though harp and harper both shall sleep;
And though no breaking chord shall raise
A note to sound our dying praise, —

No matter though we die unsung,
My poor harp broken, — all unstrung, —
Enough for us, that in our day
We woke for them our humble lay !
Enough for us, that here they deign
To listen to our humble strain !

Who'd sing for me when seventy years
Should load me with their heavy cares?
Nor Oliver nor James would then
Walk this fair earth with living men :
The sage and bard, then hand in hand,
Will walk, in love, " that better land."
" That better land ! "   Oh, can it be
That I both bard and sage shall see, —
Shall see and press the spirit-hand
Of both when in " that better land " ?
O happy thought ! and if I may,
Then quickly come that welcome day !
And may we all — a loving band —
Meet ne'er to part in " better land " !

THE GREEN, THE GOLD CORN, AND THE SHEAVES.

I.

" BETWEEN the green corn and the gold," [1]
  Between life's morning and its noon,
How many ardent loves grow cold!
  How many bright hopes cease to bloom!
How many fatal changes come,
  How many fatal truths are told,
Between life's morning and its noon, —
  " Between the green corn and the gold " !

II.

The things which pleased us when a child
  Ere noon of life neglected lie ;
Faces that in life's morning smiled
  Ere noon of life grow pale and die :
Ere noon of life life's joys are past ;
  Ere noon of life the heart grows old ;
Life's hopes and flowers all wither fast
  " Between the green corn and the gold."

[1] The first line of this poem is quoted from a very pretty little song which I have met with somewhere, but I am unable to say where, or to give its author's name now.

III.

Who has not seen the morning sun
  In blazing splendor climb the sky?
And yet, ere half his course was run,
  His darkened beams elude the eye.
Who has not seen the opening flower
  In morning splendor blooming fair?
And yet, before the noontide hour,
  Its leaves were torn, — its stem was bare.

IV.

Quick-coming clouds obscure the sun,
  Rude hands will tear the opening flower,
And human life, in joy begun,
  Is darkened ere life's noontide hour;
The brightest life will sink in gloom,
  The highest hopes grow dead and cold,
Between life's morning and its noon, —
  " Between the green corn and the gold."

V.

Between the gold corn and the sheaves, —
  The gathered sheaves of ripened grain, —
To the sad heart, life never leaves
  Enough of joy to gild its pain;
Between the noontides and the eves, —
  The solemn eves of closing life, —
Between the gold corn and the sheaves,
  Sorrow and pain alone are rife.

VI.

Then friends of early life are dead,
　Or — worse than dead — estranged and cold ;
And life's last lingering hope has fled,
　And all of life's sad tale is told.
Then the lone heart in silence grieves,
　And, breaking, sinks in death and pain :
Then the gold corn is bound in sheaves, —
　In gathered sheaves of withered grain.

THE FADED FLOWER.

(First published in " The Daily Evening Traveller.")

"What! not receive my foolish flower?
　　Nay, then, I am indeed unblest:
On me can thus thy forehead lower?
　　And knowest thou not who loves thee best?"

I.

The rose, dear maid, thou gavest to me
　　Has faded leaf by leaf,
Although I watched it tenderly,
　　And saw it fade, — with grief;
I warmed it with full many a sigh,
　　And watered it with tears;
And yet that little flower would die
　　In spite of all my cares.

II.

Its tiny stem so slenderly
　　The needed life supplied,
That though I nursed it tenderly,
　　And loved it, yet it died;

143

And as I watched its fading leaves,
   All falling one by one,
I could but feel how Hope deceives
   The while she leads us on.

III.

'Tis thus, I said, our early hopes
   Are fading day by day;
And Time's swift current never stops,
   But sweeps those hopes away.
Life's rosy morn, so sweet and fair,
   With skies so bright and gay,
Is soon o'ercast with doubt and care, —
   Our sky all cold and gray.

IV.

And early loves will fade and die,
   Howe'er the sad heart grieves,
And withered hopes around us lie,
   Like these poor withered leaves;
The heart's rich treasures soon are gone,
   All squandered one by one,
And leave the heart as cold and lone
   As winter's rayless sun.

V.

Oh, will our love thus fade away
   Or stronger grow with time?

For thee, mine strengthens day by day :
   How is it, love, with thine?
Let thy love give the life, dear maid,
   Mine give the sighs and tears ;
And then our rose shall never fade
   Through all the coming years, —

VI.

But stronger grow, and sweeter too,
   As time shall glide away ;
And, as we pass life's journey through,
   Its leaves shall ne'er decay ;
And never shall its fading bloom
   Be mourned by us at all :
Where we shall sleep, within the tomb,
   Its fragrant leaves may fall.

THESE BUDS AND FLOWERS.

ON RECEIVING A PRESENT OF ROSEBUDS AND FLOWERS ON "NEW-YEAR'S DAY."

THESE buds and flowers, from hands most dear,
Come to me with the new-born year :
They come in winter's darksome gloom
To cheer my heart with sweet perfume ;
They come upon this " New-Year's Day "
A fair one's tender wish to say,
And to my heart a tale they tell
That words could never paint so well.

These buds and flowers are dear to me,
But dearer would the giver be ;
These buds and flowers now claim my care :
The giver owns my constant prayer.
Since the fair giver comes not now,
To buds and flowers I breathe my vow ;
And, while they fade in slow decay,
For the fair giver's weal I pray.

Oh, never may this new-born year
To her bright eyes bring burning tear ;

146

And may no pains her pulses stir,
Like those I often feel for her ;
And may her heart ne'er know a gloom
Like this which now pervades my room,
While here I sit and make my moan
And sigh, — because I'm all alone !

These flowers are fair, but now to me
Far fairer would the giver be ;
These soothe the brain, whence hot tears start ;
But she could soothe the aching heart.
Of all the flowers I e'er shall see,
She is the fairest flower to me :
Then come, fair maid, and soothe my woe, —
Εγὼ σᾱς ἐξορκίζω.

LITTLE MAIDEN SWEET AND FAIR.

TO LITTLE MISS H——, FIFTEEN YEARS OLD.

"Young Peri of the West! 'tis well for me
   My years already doubly number thine;
My loveless eye unmoved may gaze on thee,
   And safely view thy ripening beauties shine,
   Happy I ne'er shall see them in decline."

LITTLE maiden sweet and fair,
Girlish face and flowing hair;
Rosebud in the early morn,
With the breath of summer born;
Violet wet with morning dew,
Tinted all with heavenly hue, —
Ere thy morning pass away,
Let me love thee while I may.

By thy airy form and grace,
By thy spirit-lighted face,
By thy clear eye's heavenly hue.
Showing heart and soul so true.
Where no touch of guile is seen,
Naught but modest maiden's mien, —
Ere thy pure looks pass away,
Let me love thee while I may.

148

Thy fair hair, all unconfined,
Floating on the summer wind,
Waves around thy tiny form
In the breath of early morn;
And thy light step, fair and free,
Shows both grace and modesty:
Ere these girlish charms decay,
Let me love thee while I may.

Thy dark tresses soon would be
Chains to bind my soul to thee;
Fairy form and girlish face
Soon will bloom with woman's grace;
Thy dark eyes and glowing cheek
Soon will love's wild language speak:
For that hour I dare not stay;
Let me love thee while I may.

May thy beauty never be
Source of after ill to thee!
May God's love protect thee here,
Fitting thee for higher sphere!
Such the prayer I pray for thee:
Some time give one tear to me:
I till death for thee will pray,
And will love thee while I may.

May thy pure soul ever be
From all sin and guile kept free!

May thy heart's true love be given
Where well prized, or else to Heaven!
May I never live to see
Sin or sorrow blighting thee,
Or thy beauties in decay!
Let me love thee, — and away.

TIME'S LESSON.

I.

TIME to me one truth has taught —
    One sad truth — long past believing ;
I have found that hearts I thought
    Truest, best, were most deceiving.

II.

I have found that one most loved,
    Dearly loved and deeply trusted,
False and wayward early proved
    To a love that should have lasted.

III.

Now this heart, once deeply thrilled
    With the keenest sense of pleasure,
Evermore with grief is filled, —
    Grief no words of song can measure.

IV.

Had she never kindly smiled,
    Had I never loved and trusted,
Had she ne'er this heart beguiled,
    Heart and hopes had ne'er been blasted.

151

v.

May that heart so dearly loved,
  Dearly loved and deeply trusted,
To some sweet remorse be moved
  By some memory which lasted!

vi.

May the pangs ruthlessly given, —
  Ruthless pangs all mutely taken, —
In eternity and heaven
  Pangs of deep repentance waken!

THERE WAS A TIME.

I.

THERE was a time those eyes of thine,
  With dear affection's tender glow,
Beamed sweetly in response to mine ;
  But now, alas ! it is not so :
Thy looks are cold, thy ways are changed ;
  For kindly words I wait in vain ;
Thy heart is cold, and all estranged,
  And seems to glory in my pain.

II.

From thy unfeeling bosom rise
  Two swelling heaps of dazzling snow,
And there, before my wondering eyes,
  Two blushing buds in beauty grow :
How can thy cold, unfeeling breast
  Nourish those rosebuds sweet and fair ?
How can they warm and sweetly rest
  When my poor heart is frozen there ?

153

III.

Oh, take thy kisses back again, —
    Kisses thy sweet lips freely gave!
Their memory loads my heart with pain,
    And buries hope within the grave;
And hide those dazzling hills of snow,
    Which, lost, would ever fairer seem:
Oh, must I those dear charms forego,
    Or is this all a fevered dream?

IV.

Oh, no, dear maid, it is not true!
    'Twas but a moody dream of mine:
Thy swelling bosom meets my view
    As warm as summer's glowing prime;
And those two rosebuds, blushing there,
    Are fairer than the buds of spring:
This world holds naught more sweet or fair
    Inspiring poet's heart to sing.

V.

So come, dear maid, and be my love;
    None other e'er shall be my bride:
If thy dear heart shall constant prove,
    I care not for the world beside;
And years may roll, and youth may fade,
    And I will live and die with thee:
So let thine eyes, my bonnie maid,
    Ne'er turn one chilling glance on me.

THE SUN OF HOPE.

I.

The sun of Hope, for one brief hour,
    Burst through the clouds of grief and woe
That wrapped my soul with darksome power,
    And warmed me with its fitful glow;
'Twas when thou bad'st me hope and love,
    And falsely swore to love in turn,
As if an angel from above
    Had taught my soul with love to burn.

II.

But when I found thee false — as fair,
    And woke from the delusive dream,
Then Hope was quenched in dark despair,
    And Desolation reigned supreme;
And Hope's bright sun in endless night
    Sank down, oh, ne'er to rise again!
And dark Despair, with magic might,
    Wound round my soul his clankless chain.

III.

And I must wear that chain for aye,
　And feel it festering round the heart,
And hide from every human eye
　Its sickening pain, its deadly smart;
And wear within the heart a grief,
　A grief untold through years of woe,
And feel that time brings no relief,
　And let no tear, in sorrow, flow.

IV.

Such the dark fate thou deal'st to me;
　And yet I bless thy hand the while,
And far from hope, and far from thee,
　In desolation seem to smile.
I viewed thee not with wanton eye:
　Mine was a more than human love;
Then, oh! in mercy. tell me why
　Thou couldst so false and wayward prove.

V.

But let it pass!　Dark years shall roll
　Alike upon thy heart and mine:
The desolation of my soul
　May yet extend itself to thine.
And yet I pray that God will spare,
　In mercy spare, thee every pain:
Let me, all uncomplaining, bear
　The bitter woe, the grief, the blame.

VI.

Let life's dark course all quickly roll :
    Oh ! would it were already o'er,
My heart at rest, and my freed soul
    Where grief and pain can come no more !
There will I wait and watch for thee ;
    And, if thy soul repentant prove,
Beyond life's dark and doubtful sea
    We yet may dwell in blissful love.

METEMPSYCHOSIS.[1]

TO MISS ——.

I.

Oh, will those bright eyes ever weep
  One crystal tear when I am low,
Or those fair lids e'er wake from sleep
  To let one tear in silence flow,
Because I ne'er may come again,
  Because my heart in death is low?
Oh God! 'twould soothe this heart's deep pain
  If I might truly deem it so.

II.

Will thy fair bosom throb with pain
  When I am cold and lowly laid,
Because I may not come again
  To cheer and love thee, pretty maid?

[1] The doctrine of the transmigration of the soul (metempsychosis) probably had its origin in Egypt. It was connected with the idea of the reward and punishment of human actions, and was taught by Pythagoras and his followers. They held, that, after death, the souls of men pass into other animal bodies; and this doctrine is still prevalent in many parts of Asia.

Oh God! 'twould soothe my aching heart
   To deem that thou dost love me so;
'Twould steal from Death his keenest dart,
   And soothe of life each bitter woe.

III.

And yet I would not have thee weep,
   Nor have thy bosom throb with pain;
Though cold in death, I could not sleep:
   My soul would fly to earth again;
And I should linger round thee here,
   Forsaking heavenly joys on high;
My soul would drink thy every tear,
   And melt in every tender sigh.

IV.

If that old-time philosophy
   By ancients taught should prove the true,
Then, by metempsychosis, I
   May change my form, not quit thy view!
Then, in that feathery songster's breast
   That cagèd hangs within thy room,
I'll nightly sing thee to thy rest,
   And nestle near thee in thy home, —

v.

And daily feel thy hand's caress,
    And thrill at thy endearing word,
As daily thou my cage shalt dress,
    Deeming thou talkest to thy bird ;
And, when thine eyes in death shall close,
    I'll fold my wings, and, closing mine,
My spirit freed shall seek repose,
    And mingle evermore with thine.

THAT SULTRY FOURTH OF JULY.

I.

Dost thou remember, dear, the time —
    That sultry fourth of July —
When fruits and flowers were in their prime,
    And I loved thee so truly?
The golden hours, on pinions bright,
    Flew o'er me and my Zara:
The memory of that deep delight
    No time or change can vary.

II.

I culled thee fruits, I brought sweet flowers
    And twined them with thy tresses,
And heeded not the fleeting hours,
    But heeded thy caresses.
Ah, woe is me! why did those hours
    Fly with such ruthless fleetness?
Oh, could ye not, ye heavenly powers,
    Prolong them and their sweetness?

161

III.

I never, never shall forget
    How all the lengthening shadows
Closed round us when the sun had set,
    Concealing hills and meadows ;
And how I held thee to my heart
    That long, sweet hour of parting :
Oh, pleasures past bring present smart,
    And these sad tears now starting !

IV.

When will another day, sweet maid,
    Beam with such hours of gladness ?
Why do past joys now cast a shade
    So much akin to sadness ?
Why does fond memory always bring
    Thoughts of that day's deep pleasure ?
Why to it does the fond heart cling
    As to some long-lost treasure ?

V.

Well, time may fly, and years may roll,
    And joys and pains may vary ;
But never, never shall my soul
    Forget the charms of Zara !
And, till life's latest sun is set,
    I e'er shall love thee truly ;
And, oh ! I never will forget
    That sultry fourth of July !

HEAVEN'S ARTILLERY, OR WAR AND PEACE.

I.

How the hot, burning sun
 Fiercely doth blaze,
While, in his course half-run,
 Darting his rays!
Hung high in the zenith
 O'er forest and field,
To mortals he seemeth
 Like God's mighty shield.

II.

Like God's mighty shield there,
 Inviting to war,
While the hot, sultry air
 Blazes afar;
And all the wilting trees,
 Bowing the head,
Sigh for the cooling breeze,
 Stifled and dead.

III.

Now the black thunder-clouds
  Rise from afar,
And, like to armèd crowds
  Ready for war,
Close up their serried ranks,
  Heavy and dark ;
Rise from those thunder-banks
  Mutterings stark.

IV.

On they move steadily,
  Slowly at first ;
More and more readily, —
  Soon they shall burst !
Deep-rolling thunder and
  Banners unrolled
Waken the wonder and
  Fear of the world !

V.

Wheeling now rapidly,
  Fearless and stark ;
Now mingling vapidly,
  Heavy and dark :
Then, in a moment, they
  Close o'er the sun,
Quenching his burning ray :
  Battle's begun !

VI.

Now the red lightning-flash,
   Fearlessly hurled,
Wakes the loud thunder-crash,
   Shaking the world!
Rapidly darting now
   Flash upon flash!
Loud thunders starting, — how
   Dreadful the crash!

VII.

Never could mortals,
   In death or in life,
Wake from War's portals
   Such horrible strife:
All the dark fiends of hell,
   Mingling in war,
Charging with shout and yell,
   Wake not such jar.

VIII.

How the black masses wheel,
   Mingle, and roar!
How the loud-crashing peal
   Sounds the world o'er!
Elements God unbinds
   Leap into life,
And the wild, roaring winds
   Join in the strife.

IX.

Red lightnings flashing
    The universe o'er ;
Loud thunders crashing
    With deafening roar ;
The big rain is pouring
    A deluge to earth ;
Heaven's elements, roaring,
    Give Chaos new birth.

X.

How long can the heavens and
    Earth thus endure?
Will not God's mighty hand
    Make us secure?
Yes, lo where the bow of
    His promise unfurled
Brings hope, and a show of
    His love for the world !

XI.

Elements warring, now
    Cease at His will ;
Dark clouds retiring, now
    Thunders are still ;
Shines forth His sun again
    With softened ray :
Ever, in joy or pain,
    Unto Him pray !

MEMORIES OF CHILDHOOD.

LINES WRITTEN ON REVISITING THE HOME OF MY
CHILDHOOD IN WILLIAMSTOWN, VT., AFTER YEARS
OF ABSENCE.

> " And other days come back on me
> With recollected music, though the tone
> Is changed and solemn, like the cloudy groan
> Of dying thunder on the distant wind."
>
> *Childe Harold.*

I.

Once more I revisit the land of my birth,
And seek the loved cottage and home-hallowed
    hearth,
Where, a frolicsome band from anxiety free,
We gathered in youth round a dear mother's knee.

II.

Where now is that brotherly-sisterly band?
Estranged, and all scattered afar through the land;
And where is that mother, so loved and so dear?
Oh, stay, while I water her grave with a tear!

167

III.

Oh, never did God, in his mercy and truth,
Give a better or dearer to childhood and youth!
I breathe o'er her grave many prayer-laden sighs,
While the hot, burning tears pour like rain from the
    eyes.

IV.

Oh God! if I only could see her again
With these eyes that are reddened with weeping and
    pain,
And tell her how terribly dark was our home,
And how saddened was life when she left us alone!

V.

I have placed o'er her grave the white marble to tell
Her dear name, and the reason we loved her so well;
And have left by her side ample room, where, in
    time,
My ashes shall mingle, dear mother, with thine!

VI.

And, oh! if thy spirit hath power to come,
When my spirit is freed from this temporal home,
Then come, dearest mother, and guide me afar
To thy own spirit-home on some beautiful star!

VII.

Our cottage has crumbled and gone to decay,
And dark weeds and brambles have choked up the
  way;
But the darkest of weeds are the weeds of the heart,
And the brambles of thought pierce the soul like a
  dart.

VIII.

The threshold is broken, the hearthstone is bare,
Where, at evening and bedtime, we all said our
  prayer,
As each one, in turn, kissed dear mother "good-
  night,"
And clambered to bed with hearts happy and light.

IX.

Where are the familiar old faces and forms
That loved us in sunshine, and cheered us in storms?
I search the old places, and call them in vain;
For only sad Echo replies to each name.

X.

And e'en the old schoolhouse seems altered and
  changed,
Like faces once loved that have long been estranged;
The brook still goes by it with musical flow, —
But a music how changed from the dear long ago!

XI.

And where are the voices that greeted the ear,
When, belated at morn, I came hurrying here?
And where is the teacher, so faithful and true,
Who even our errors with kindness could view?

XII.

Those voices are hushed, and the teacher is gone;
Here I wander, in sadness and silence, alone,
And sigh for the friends of the dear long ago,
And mingle my tears with the brook in its flow.

XIII.

My dear native land, I must bid thee adieu,
And all the loved spots which in boyhood I knew!
My heart with unbearable sorrow is moved
When I mark the sad changes in homes which I
    loved.

XIV.

Thy hills and thy valleys, so dear to my heart,
'Tis painful to view them, and painful to part;
How I loved, in my youth, all the glories of shade
That thy wide-waving woodlands in summer once
    made!

XV.

Thy mountains are green, as thy name doth imply,[1]
And in picturesque beauty with any may vie;
And with my loved country what land can compare
When the perfumes of autumn embalm thy sweet
     air, —

XVI.

When thy woodlands are tinted brown, purple, and
     red,
And thy mantle of autumn is everywhere spread,
Where the scarlet and yellow are mingled with green
In colors as gorgeous as ever were seen?

XVII.

O land of sweet lakes and of wild mountain-rills,
Of wide-waving woodlands and purple-crowned hills!
Thy maidens are fair, and thy yeomen are brave,
And thy soil could ne'er nourish the soul of a slave.[2]

XVIII.

Thy mothers are noble; thy warriors were brave
As the bravest that struggled their country to save;
And may God, in his mercy, from danger and harm
For ever protect them with his mighty arm!

[1] Vermont derives its name from two French words, *vert mont;* i.e.,
"green mountain."

[2] There was never a slave owned in the State of Vermont. The first
constitution of the State prohibited slavery.

XIX.

And all thy dear maidens, so lovely and fair,
With white, swelling bosoms and long, waving hair,
May some worthier bard to their praise give his
    breath
When my harp and my harpings are silent in
    death, —

XX.

And I join the great throng of the harpers of old,
Where the mightiest bards their high harpings shall
    hold,
And I sit at their feet, all enraptured, to hear
Their golden-toned lyres in heaven's bright sphere!

THE HEART THAT IN SILENCE IS BREAKING.

"The day drags through, though storms keep out the sun;
And thus the heart will break, yet brokenly live on!"

I.

THE heart that in silence is breaking
   Is most to be pitied of all;
When, alone in its desolate aching,
   It drinks of the wormwood and gall.
Surrounded by beings called human,
   Yet never, among them, from one —
Not even from pitying woman —
   Doth mercy or sympathy come.

II.

As seen on some desolate mountain,
   One lonely and lightning-scathed pine
That is fed by no nourishing fountain,
   There biding in silence its time,
So the heart, that in silence is breaking,
   Unnourished by pity or love,
In desolate loneliness aching,
   Hopes only for rest from above.

173

III.

There are moments when memory, waking,
  The scenes of the past will recall;
When the heart, in its loneliness breaking,
  Craves mercy and pity from all;
When the desolate soul is surrounded
  By darkness unbroken and drear,
Or the sad heart most deeply is wounded
  By one of all others most dear.

IV.

Then, oh! if the beings called human
  Would mercy and sympathy lend,
Or the God-given angel called woman
  Would o'er us in truthfulness bend,
It would be to the soul like nepenthe
  By pitying angels shed round,
As if God in His mercy had sent me
  A balm for the soul's every wound.

V.

Oh God! do I err in believing
  That somewhere on earth may be found
One being, who, never deceiving,
  Shall solace and soothe every wound?
In whom the dark soul, in confiding
  Its sorrows, shall sympathy find?
Where mercy and truth, all-abiding,
  Shall solace one tempest-tossed mind?

VI.

Oh! will they for ever pursue me,
  Like vultures pursuing their prey?
For ever still strive to undo me,
  Whatever of them I may say?
Ah, yes! they will seek to defame me,
  Much rather than cherish and love;
And, sooner than praise, they would blame me,
  However to them I might prove.

VII.

My faults! — well, I know they are many,
  And deeply I mourn for them all;
Yet, though I had never shown any,
  Not less would they strive for my fall.
Oh! would they but search with slight labor,
  Some errors at home might be seen;
But "the mote" in the eye of our neighbor
  Hides always in ours "the beam." [1]

VIII.

But let them war on at their pleasure,
  The many pursuing the one!
For God, in His justice, will measure
  The right and the wrong that is done;

[1] "And why beholdest thou the mote that is in thy brother's eye, but considerest not the beam that is in thine own eye?

"Or how wilt thou say to thy brother, Let me pull out the mote out of thine eye; and behold a beam is in thine own eye?

"Thou hypocrite, first cast out the beam out of thine own eye, and then shalt thou see clearly to cast out the mote out of thy brother's eye."
  Matt. vii. 3–5.

Yes, God, in His wisdom, is making
A note of each sparrow's sad fall;[1]
And the heart that in silence is breaking
May win as much mercy as all!

[1] "Are not two sparrows sold for a farthing? and one of them shall not fall on the ground without your Father.

"Fear ye not therefore, ye are of more value than many sparrows."

Matt. x. 29–31.

"There is a special providence in the fall of a sparrow."

Hamlet, Act v. Scene 2.

TO MISS ——.

I.

This little casket, rich and rare,
With girlish face so sweet and fair,
To me is sweeter, dearer far
Than queenly pride and jewels are.

II.

Yet take it back! it gives deep pain
To my sad heart and throbbing brain;
For, while I gaze, I sadly feel
The change that time must there reveal.

III.

Oh! couldst thou linger as thou art,
With girlish face and girlish heart,
Just on the verge of womanhood,
Where every withered dame once stood, —

177

IV.

Then would I hail thee as divine;
Then would I clasp and keep thee mine:
Not all the powers of earth should tear
From my embrace a gift so rare.

V.

And thy fair tresses, unconfined,
Now waving in the summer wind,
Strong chains and fetters then should be
To bind my loving soul to thee.

VI.

Oh, that some god the gift would give
To bid thy girlish beauty live!
It may not be: Time wings his flight;
Thy day is waning into night.

VII.

For amulet of safety, bind
Thy soul to knowledge! store thy mind
With sages' songs that bards sublime
Chant to us from the olden time!

VIII.

Then, when thy summer days are past,
And thy heart feels the chilling blast
Of age's winter, they shall be
Sources of deepest joy to thee.

IX.

And I for amulet will wear
This fair, sweet face with flowing hair,
Bound to my heart in every clime,
Through every change of place and time.

X.

Happy that I may ne'er behold
Thy sweet smile fade, thy face grow old,
But e'er remember thee thus fair
With girlish face and flowing hair.

STANZAS.

I.

Why wilt thou wound the heart that loved thee so?
Why bring upon it all this bitter woe?
Why grieve the heart whose every thought for thee
Was love and tenderness and constancy?

II.

The day may come when thou, in turn, shalt know
The bitter pangs of an enduring woe,
When thou for one heart's truthful love wilt pine,
Such as thou knewest in the olden time.

III.

When that day comes, oh, sometimes think of me!
Think of my heart's deep, earnest love for thee;
Think of the olden and the happy time
When I was all to thee, — when thou wert mine.

IV.

Then in thy heart there may arise a pain,
A secret wish that I may come again, —
May yet return in truthfulness to thee
From my long pilgrimage beyond the sea.

180

ETHEL GREY.

(Fragment from an Unpublished Poem.)

Oh ! many a weary year ago —
 How many I dare not say —
A maiden lived, whom you may know
 By the name of Ethel Grey.

But where her home, and who her love,
 It suits me not to say ;
For she is now in heaven above,
 And he is far away.

Enough, to know they lived and loved,
 And ne'er can love again ;
Enough, to know one faithless proved,
 And one now bears the pain.

  .   .   .   .

In the churchyard, far away,
Sleeps the form of Ethel Grey ;
There, beneath the cold gray stone,
In cold sleep she sleepeth on.

With her pale hands, o'er her breast,
Folded in their final rest,
Underneath the spreading tree,
In her last sleep, sleepeth she.

Through the branches all the day
Flecks of golden sunlight stray ;
And her silent, simple grave
In their golden beauty bathe.

Through the sad night's silent hours
Moonbeams pale incrust the flowers,
Which, upon her little grave,
In the winds of summer wave.

Thus, while years steal on apace,
Rests she in her resting-place ;
Moldering in the solemn tomb,
Waiting there the trump of doom, —

Which shall break her silent sleep,
Calling her to wake and weep,
Where all truths are open laid
For betrayer and betrayed, —

There to meet the certain doom
Waiting all beyond the tomb,
There to bow beneath the rod
Of a just, all-seeing God.

.   .   .   .

Reader, ponder well, and be
Thy heart from all guile kept free !
And, when tempted to betray,
Pause, and think of Ethel Grey !

THE POWER OF SONG.

TO ———.

I.

THE power of song within me lies. —
The godlike power of song!
And I will wake its symphonies
As time shall roll along;
I'll wake a strain to reach thine ear,
Which, wondering, thou shalt turn to hear.

II.

And immortality — in song —
The boon I thee will give!
For, by thy name twined in my song,
Thy memory shall live!
And millions yet unborn shall see
The story of my love for thee.

III.

And when long weary years shall roll
Sadly o'er thee and me,
And the bright visions of thy soul
Have faded mournfully,
Then o'er our past turn back thine eye,
And owe me immortality!

184

THE FRIARS GRAY.

I.

I ENVY them, those friars gray!
They rose at earliest dawn of day,
And, with their holy matin-song,
Ushered the new-born day along.

II.

And then, in cloisters quaint and gray,
Mused the long summer hours away,
Till, with the setting sun of even,
The holy vesper-song was given.

III.

Then, for the dying and the dead,
The midnight Mass was sung or said;
While tapers, burning faint and low,
Scarce served the sleeping dead to show.

IV.

Thus passed their solemn lives away
In old cathedrals quaint and gray,

Like hermits in a living tomb,
Where dead and living both find room.

v.

And thus would I avoid the strife
And turmoil of this weary life,
And in the cloisters, quaint and gray,
Would muse and meditate and pray, —

vi.

Where pride and fashion ne'er could come
To wound me in my solemn home,
And wild ambition never there
Could mingle with my humble prayer.

vii.

And there the glance of Beauty's eye,
Disarmed, should harmless pass me by,
And Beauty's glowing form should be
For evermore as dead to me.

viii.

Thus living, I prepared might be
To hail " that day of wrath " with glee, —
" *Dies iræ, dies illa*
Solvet sæclum in favilla."

THE MORNING WALK.

'Tis sweet the towering hill to climb
In the fresh glow of morning prime,
And sweet the haunts of men to leave,
Nature's untainted breath to breathe,
And seek the vocal woodlands wide
Where Nature glows in pristine pride.
I love some sylvan haunt to tread
Where the broad branches overhead
Stretch their weird arms 'twixt heaven and me,
And clap their hands in leafy glee,
While yet the dew is on the grass
Sparkling like diamonds as I pass ;
And, while I muse in woodland vale,
I love to hear the plaintive tale
Of gentle thrush and blackbird gay
In unpremeditated lay
Pouring, in sweetest strains of love,
Their grateful praise to God above, —
A purer and a sweeter praise
Than sinful man can ever raise.
And here, on many a morn of spring,
I've roamed to hear the sweet birds sing,

And listened to the mellow note
Poured from the bluebird's muffled throat,
And found in Nature's woodlands wild
Companionship for Nature's child ;
And here, on many a summer eve,
I've loitered, loath to take my leave,
While night's dark shades of deepened gloom
Have wrapped me in a living tomb,
Till through mysterious, endless space
God's wondrous stars stood forth in place,
Drawing the heart and soul and eye
From things below to One on high.

THE EVENING WALK.

When the great sun in golden glow
On purple couch is sinking low,
And, through the quivering heats of day,
The western breezes softly play,
'Tis sweet the stifled town to leave,
The cooling woodland airs to breathe,
And, with some fair one by our side,
To roam the country far and wide.
'Tis sweet the wayside fence to climb,
To pluck the rose and eglantine,
And bear them to our waiting fair,
And twine them with her raven hair,
And watch the tender, love-lit smile
That lights her heavenly face the while.
And if some envious, wicked thorn
The hand which culled the flower hath torn,
With pin, drawn forth from graceful robe,
All tenderly the wound she'll probe ;
And, though the wound may smart with pain,
We can but wish it probed again :
For ne'er was " balm of Gilead " found
Like her soft touch for throbbing wound.

189

Let cynics smile, and toss the head,
Because with them all love is dead;
But never yet beat manly heart
Where woman could not claim a part,
And Eden's garden was but sad
Till woman came to make it glad.
So let cold critics say their say,
While we, with sweet love, live our day,
And, with our fair one by our side,
Roam the green fields at eventide;
And cull the rose and eglantine.
With her fair, flowing locks to twine;
And feel the smart from envious thorn,
And solace by her soft touch borne;
And drink rich draughts of love and pain
Through hours which ne'er may come again:
While on Love's altars, freely laid,
Youth's untold wealth of love is paid!

THE BROKEN VOW.[1]

" Rammentati! ne stringe il cielo! e amor."

I.

By the oaths that once were plighted
  In the sight of God above ;
By the hopes that once were lighted
  By the promises of love ; —

II.

By the God who reigns above thee ;
  By the heaven we hope to gain ;
By the demons who could move thee
  To thy perjury and shame ; —

III.

Can thy unkept vows betoken
  Aught of peace to thee or me?
Doth thine oath in heaven, broken,
  Promise future bliss to thee?

[1] First published in the Daily Evening Traveller.

IV.

Oh! from out the past a starker
    Phantom-form shall soon appear,
And ever o'er thy heart a darker
    Shadow bend from year to year!

V.

For thy heart yet holds a treasure,
    Hoarded by thy willing will, —
Memories of each by-gone pleasure,
    Memories thou canst not kill.

VI.

And the Past, yet in a deeper
    Prophet's tones, shall speak to thee,
Awaking in thy heart a sleeper
    Who will whisper oft of me.

VII.

And thy broken oaths shall bend thee
    To thy tomb with magic power;
And the future ne'er shall lend thee
    Hope or solace in that hour.

VIII.

But the past shall ever send thee
    Tokens of thy broken vow;
And the few, who now commend thee,
    Shall prove false, as thou art now.

SONG: I'LL DREAM OF THEE.

(Lines for Music.)

I.

I'LL dream, I'll dream of thee, love;
    I'll dream we ne'er had met,
Or, having been with thee, love,
    We were not parted yet.

II.

I'll clasp within my arms, love,
    Thy fancied form so fair,
And gaze upon thy charms, love,
    Till vanished into air.

III.

And then I'll weep for thee, love;
    When waking from that dream
Thy fancied form shall flee, love,
    With morning's early beam.

IV.

I'll curse returning day, love,
  That steals thee from my arms,
And for the midnight pray, love,
  And thy returning charms.

V.

And if the years should roll, love.
  And we ne'er meet again,
Oh, then my very soul, love,
  Will sink in endless pain!

VI.

And I shall never cease, love.
  To weep and pray for thee,
Until, in endless peace, love,
  Our spirits joined shall be.

STANZAS.

TO ———.

I.

Ere the passing day is done,
Ere goes down the evening sun,
Ere that sun shall rise again,
I shall be upon the main ;
But, though now from thee I flee.
Shall my spirit be with thee ;
And in future thou shalt feel
What thy heart would not reveal.

II.

For. when moonbeams cold and still
Sleep on meadow, lake, and hill,
And when evening breezes play,
Strangely soft. their evening lay,
Then a weird and mystic spell
Shall upon thy spirit dwell ;
And thou shalt in sorrow feel
What thy heart would not reveal.

III.

And when Pleasure's cup is full,
And thy heart with pride doth swell, —
When, in mazy dance and song,
Thou art worshiped by the throng, —
Then, within thy heart and brain,
Thou shalt feel a secret pain ;
And, from halls where pleasures keep,
Thou wilt turn away to weep.

IV.

In the calm and in the storm,
In the night and in the morn,
And at twilight's holy hour,
Thou shalt feel my spirit's power ;
And, when memories of the past
On thy brain come crowding fast,
Then thou mayst in sorrow know
'Twas not well to give the blow.

V.

For a strange and secret dread
E'er shall linger round thy bed ;
And, when in thy troubled sleep
Thou dost start and wake and weep,
Then, at midnight's dreaded hour,
Thou shalt own my spirit's power ;
And the sorrow thou wilt feel
Shall a hidden truth reveal.

VI.

Thou shalt find, yet find too late,
That thy heart is desolate ;
Thou shalt know, yet know in vain,
That thou canst not love again ;
And this deep and hidden spell
E'er shall on thy spirit dwell ;
And the future, that must be,
Ne'er can bring relief to thee.

VII.

Thus a spirit of the past
Shall teach thee thine own heart at last,
And in madness thou shalt dare
Demons in fantastic prayer ;
But an arm thou canst not see
Ever shall encircle thee ;
And a prayer, by thee unheard,
E'er shall plead for thee with God.

MY BARK ROCKS IN THE BAY BELOW.

When on the eve of setting sail for Europe, the author addressed the following lines to his youthful friend, Henry P. Leland of Philadelphia, —a younger brother of the poet, Charles G. Leland,—a young gentleman of the rarest attainments, whose early years gave promise of a future success which might even rival the growing fame of his gifted brother; but, by some unaccountable dispensation of Providence, his brilliant mind became early overclouded, and almost in the freshness of youth he was called away "to that undiscovered country from whose bourne no traveler returns."

I.

My bark rocks in the bay below ;
　　The winds blow gently off the shore :
But, Leland, ere from thee I go,
　　Let's quaff a social glass once more.

II.

Then I am off to other climes ;
　　And many a year, I ween, will pass
Ere I with thee renew these times,
　　Or drink with thee a social glass.

III.

So fill once more the flowing bowl,
  And here — our parting faith to prove —
Come, pledge me with thy heart and soul:
  Our toast is Woman, wine, and love.

IV.

Be woman's smiles for ever thine, —
  Smiles bright as those of saints above!
Be thy cup filled with richest wine!
  Be thy heart bound in chains of love!

V.

Whatever Fate may deal to me,
  Where'er my unloved life may end,
May God in mercy prosper thee!
  May happiness thy life attend!

VI.

But sometimes, when thy cup of life
  Runs o'er with every earthly bliss,
One moment turn from friend or wife,
  And from that hour think back to this.

VII.

Think of the hours when thou and I
    In boyish years wove day-dreams bright;
Think of our past with constant sigh,
    Think of our parting here to-night!

VIII.

And, if one tear-drop in thine eye
    Trembles at thought of days of yore,
Then, if to me thou giv'st one sigh,
    I ask no more! I ask no more!

IX.

So fare thee well! and, while I roam
    Apart from thee in foreign clime,
I'll ever think of those at home,
    And ever drink to thee and thine.

MUSINGS.

When the hours of day are gone,
And the evening shades come on,
To night's thoughtful hours I go,
Musing o'er this life of woe;
And, within my room alone,
Listening to the night-wind's moan,
As the wintry storm sweeps by
Blotting moon and stars from sky,
Thoughtfully I sit and gaze
At the cheerful fire's blaze,
And the ghostlike shadows tall
Flitting round upon the wall;
Watch them come and go again,
Like the phantoms of the brain,
With their muffled feet beneath,
Like the witches of the heath.
Sitting thus in dreamy mood,
Musing o'er the bad and good
That befell me from the time
I started in my boyhood's prime, —
Pursuing all the wildest schemes
Ever dreamt in madcap's dreams, —

Now I view with little joy
What so pleased me when a boy;
For bright visions all are gone
With our manhood's early dawn,
And we mourn our boyhood spent
In a world of discontent.
Things that unto boyhood seem
Brilliant as a fairy dream
Fade with manhood's dawn away;
Golden morning turns to gray!
Life itself is but a dream:
Things are never what they seem, —
Unsubstantial phantoms all,
Like these shadows on the wall.

TO ANNA,

This accomplished young lady — afterwards the wife of a gentleman now eminent as judge of a court of the United States — was early sung (by "angel voices") to her final rest.

I.

Accept the gift
Which in all kindness unto thee I send,
And deem it sent thee by thy truest friend;
And may it lift
Thy spirit up from earth and earthly things
To soar in lands of song on Fancy's wings!

II.

And may it be
Ever a source of hidden joy to thee,
Lighting thy pathway to that boundless sea,
The grave, when he
Who in his boyhood gave it is no more,
Or wanders friendless on some foreign shore.

III.

Oh, may " the voices "
Speak unto thee in murmurs soft and low,
Soothing with gentle tones thy hours of woe !
And when rejoices
Thy heart with hidden joy, may they then be
" Familiar voices " of calm joy to thee !

IV.

And when long years
Have cast their shadows on thy heart's decay,
And friends of youth have sadly passed away,
May bitter tears
Be strangers to thee, and this friend remain
To sing to thee an old familiar strain !

V.

But when at last
The heart grows sear with grief, and all is gone,
And Death walks sternly in to claim his own,
Oh, may the Past
Look smilingly upon thee, and at last
May " angel voices " sing thee to thy rest !

THE APOLOGY.

TO SARAH D——.

The very estimable young lady to whom these lines were addressed fell an early victim — as did also a younger sister — to that scourge of our New England climate, consumption; leaving one older sister, now the accomplished wife of an ex-governor of the Commonwealth, to mourn their untimely loss.

I.

Forgive me, Sarah, if, when last we met,
　My tones were altered, or my looks unkind ;
'Twas melancholy's curse on my soul set,
　The curse of sorrow on my shadowy mind.

II.

For I have suffered wrongs, deep, unforgiven ;
　Have seen each loved one coldly turn away,
Had young hopes blighted and young friendships
　　riven, —
　Friendship ! even ours was well-nigh lied away.

III.

O'er things like these the soul will darkly brood.
  And melancholy then steals o'er the heart;
And often in my wildest, mirthful mood,
  These thoughts come o'er me, and all joys depart.

IV.

But unto thee I bear no thought unkind;
  Far from unkind, the looks which thee I give:
Thy form hath long been imaged in my mind. —
  Forgive these few words, Sarah dear. forgive.

V.

Oh, have I ever given thy bosom pain,
  Or caused thee e'er one sorrowing tear to know.
'Twill bow my saddened soul with hidden pain,
  And fill too full the measure of my woe.

GIVE ME BACK MY BREAKING HEART.

TO OPHELIA.[1]

"Had we never lov'd sae kindly,
Had we never lov'd sae blindly,
Never met — or never parted,
We had ne'er been broken-hearted."

BURNS.

I.

LADY, ere the tie we sever
(Which I ween should bind for ever),
Ere that tie thou darest to break,
Hear the last request I make :

[1] The real name of this young lady was not Ophelia; but we often called her so, in view of her unhappy destiny. The daughter of an eminent New England clergyman, — young, handsome, and accomplished, — she had been affianced, against her expressed wishes, through the determined persuasion of a stern father, to a man (also a clergyman) far older than herself, and of a stern and unbending disposition, without either personal attractions or mental congeniality to draw her towards him. And under these circumstances we first met at the house of, mutual friends, while she was passing the last summer of her freedom in the country; and where both were young, — for neither had then seen twenty years, — and one was beautiful, it was not strange that a warm, though juvenile, attachment soon grew up, which, at the hour of parting, gave occasion for the foregoing little song. It need hardly be said that the young lady's married life with the husband of her father's choice was not of the happiest, and has since been one of strange vicissitudes.

If thou wouldst not give me sorrow
Which can know no peace of morrow,
Then, " fayre ladye," ere we part,
Give me back my breaking heart !

II.

By the powers which are above me,
" Gentle ladye," I have loved thee,
And my love was pure for thee,
From all shade of passion free :
But the Fates now do us sever, —
Parted we must be for ever :
Go thou to him of whom they speak ;
I go, forgetfulness to seek.

III.

I know him not of whom they tell ;
He may not love thee half as well :
His love, as brother's, true may be,
That, ten times told, is mine for thee !
But let it pass ; I wish thee joy,
Nor with my presence will annoy ;
And, since thy love was not for me,
My prayer may be for him and thee.

IV.

'Twould soothe to press that lip of thine
In fondness once again to mine,
And take one painful, parting view,
And breathe to thee one fond adieu ;
But I must strive, although in vain,
Never to think of thee again,
And wander far from thee — alone :
I'm going, " fayre one ! " I am gone.

TO MARY, DEPARTED.

(From Juvenile Poems.)

I.

ALAS, thou art gone where the cold grave doth bind
thee,
    And the cold arms of Death now encircle thee
round!
While the friends of thy youth, left in sorrow behind thee,
    Are mourning for Mary now cold in the ground.

II.

The pride of the village in which thou didst dwell,
    While the few years sped by that were given thee
here, —
All the villagers long will remember thee well,
    And give to thy memory many a tear.

III.

Oh, why did the cold hand of Death touch a flower
    That bloomed in the garden of Nature so fair?
Could not man's invention, his prayers, or his power
    Compel the grim monster the treasure to spare?

210

IV.

Ah, no! all that poor mortal man could accomplish
To nourish and cherish that flower, he did;
And yet its fair form did the tyrant demolish, —
It was not for mortals the deed to forbid.

V.

Alas, thou art gone! and the green turf above thee
Lies cold on the bosom that once was so fair,
And the friends of thy youth who so fondly did love
thee
Lean over thy young grave, and weep in despair.

VI.

But neither their prayers nor their tears can recall
thee:
Thou hast gone to that land from whence none
can return;
And morning and eve, when in fondness they call
thee,
The echo will answer, " She sleeps 'neath the urn."

VII.

And, oh! never again, round the hearthstone at eve,
Can her bright, sunny smiles lend their influence
there;
For she from among you has taken her leave,
And ye ne'er can behold more that maiden so fair.

VIII.

When years have rolled by, and by some she's for-
　　got, —
　　Though few who e'er saw will forget that fair
　　　　maid, —
Then the villagers ever will point out the spot
　　Where Mary, the pride of their village, was laid.

IX.

Alas, fare thee well! for we ne'er more can meet,
　　And I never again can behold thy sweet face;
But thy mem'ry will long in my heart hold its seat:
　　Until time is no more it will there have a place.

OH, ASK ME NOT WHEN I AM SAD!

(From Juvenile Poems.)

I.

Oh, ask me not, when I am sad,
  Why care sits heavy on my brow!
Oh, ask me not, when I am glad,
  What pleasures light my spirit now!

II.

For I have thoughts thou canst not know;
  Have griefs e'en thou must fail to share;
Have hours of bliss and hours of woe, —
  Dark hours of thought and anxious care.

III.

And often in my wildest mood,
  Back to my heart and to my brain,
When dance and song go gayly round,
  Dark thoughts come flowing back again.

IV.

So ask me not, when I am sad,
  Why care sits heavy on my brow ;
And ask me not, when I am glad,
  What pleasures light my spirit now.

V.

For thy young heart could never bear
  The woes which early come to me ;
But thou wilt teach my lip to wear
  A smile if I am dear to thee.

FAREWELL TO MY LITTLE SCHOOLMATE.

(From Juvenile Poems.)

I.

FAREWELL! and, if it be decreed
    That we for ever part,
Accept a blessing ere thou goest
    From my sad, aching heart.

II.

When thou art gone, and I alone
    At evening o'er the lea
Shall wander forth, as oft before
    I've sported there with thee, —

III.

Remembrance then will start a tear:
    That tear will flow for thee.
Oh! will those melting eyes of thine
    E'er shed one tear for me?

IV.

Ay, fare thee well! but, ere thou goest
　　With dearer friends to dwell,
Accept a blessing from the lips
　　Which, quivering, say, " Farewell ! "

V.

Older heads, perhaps, would tell thee
　　More than I have learned to speak ;
But the unspoken truth is plainer
　　On my burning, boyish cheek.

VI.

Oh ! when we have both grown older,
　　When our school-days all are o'er,
Wilt thou sometimes, then, remember
　　One whom thou wilt see no more?

THE SUMMER DAYS OF '81.

TO ——.

> " Dear as remembered kisses after death,
>   And sweet as those by hopeless fancy feigned
>   On lips that are for others; deep as love,
>   Deep as first love, and wild with all regret;
>   O death in life! the days that are no more."
>   TENNYSON.

I.

THE summer days of '81
  Rolled sweetly by for thee and me,
And not a cloud obscured the sun
  That warmed our love and constancy;
But now the waning year proclaims
  Those summer days for ever fled,
And the hoarse wind's low, mournful strains
  Sound like sad dirges o'er the dead.

II.

The golden-rod beside the way
  Has parted with its brilliant hue,
And dusty milkweed-pods display
  Their down and ripened seeds to view;

And autumn crickets load the air
   Of evening with a mournful tone,
And where the summer roses were
   The autumn winds are making moan.

III.

And falling leaves and faded flowers
   Speak sadly to my boding heart;
To me their fate presages ours,
   When thou and I and hope must part.
I know the coming years will roll
   Often with darkly clouded sun,
But never from my constant soul
   Shall fade the lights of '81.

IV.

Thy heart can never know the pain
   Which thrills me to the bosom's core,
When, parting, ne'er to meet again,
   We say adieu for evermore!
Dark years may come to thee and me,
   And hope may die ere life is done,
But ne'er shall fade from memory
   The sunny days of '81.

TO HENRY W. LONGFELLOW,

ON HIS SEVENTY-FIFTH BIRTHDAY.

Astra regunt homines! sed regit astra Deus!

The following poem — composed to celebrate the natal day of New England's greatest poet — was sent to Mr. Longfellow on his seventy-fifth birthday, Feb. 27, 1882. And, although the writer is not a believer in what are usually called presentiments, yet, in truthfulness, he must confess, that, at the time of sending it, he was solemnly impressed with the feeling that it was to be the last birthday that Mr. Longfellow was ever to pass. And in view of the fact that he died in less than a month thereafter, though in usual health on his last birthday, some lines in the poem would seem to have been almost prophetic in their sad foreshadowings.

ANOTHER! ay, another year
Rolls o'er thy head, O Poet dear!
O Poet! dear to every heart
That e'er felt thrill of poet's art,
And doubly dear to hearts that long
Have thrilled in echo to thy song, —
Thy song! thy many songs of love,
Which float around us and above,
Like "spirits of the viewless air,"
Shedding their holy influence where
The fainting souls of toiling men,
Cheered by their voice, take heart again.

Thy " Psalm of Life " doth strength impart
To many a tried and troubled heart,
To many a weary foot that tries,
In vain, by patient toil to rise, —
To rise and climb the shining way
Which thou didst tread in youthful day.

But what a toilsome road they find,
When, lacking thy majestic mind,
They seek to climb the upward way
Where thou didst soar to light and day !
And some, who thought like thee to soar,
Sink by the way to rise no more ;
Yet few, — oh, very few indeed ! —
Still toiling, hope for better meed,
And, taking heart from thine own lay,
Still struggle on the upward way ;
And, " with a heart for any fate,"
They " learn to labor and to wait."

To such thy name and fame are dear ;
And, while they view thee year by year
Throned o'er New England's realm of song,
Pray that thy years be lengthened long, —
Yet, praying, listening, ever fear
The coming death dirge-notes to hear ;
For well we know that time sweeps on,
Like " the storm-wind Euroclydon,"

And with a power of mighty force
Bears all before it in its course.
And yet we pray that years may be
In plenty still bestowed on thee,
And that for many a year we may
Still hail with joy thy natal day;
Yet, oh! there ever lingers still
A doubt, a fear of coming ill, —
A fear lest the sweet dream should break,
And our sad souls to sorrow wake, —
A fear lest the stern " reaper " come
The ripened grain to garner home.

When that day comes, as come it must,
With its stern fiat, " Dust to dust! "
When thy sun, sinking in the west,
Shall close thy day, and thou shalt rest, —
Oh, what a direful, woeful day
For those who watch its setting ray!
And what a wail of grief shall rise
To waft thy spirit to the skies!
And what a cloud of woe shall bend
O'er all when thy sweet life shall end!
Millions of sobs will then combine
To mourn thee, — none more deep than mine.

New England's harp will sound a wail
To load New England's every gale!

And every hill and every vale
Shall echo back its dying wail!
And hearts shall bow, and eyes shall weep,
When thy loved form in death shall sleep!
The Muse, beholding thee expire,
Shall weep above her broken lyre!

On that sad day, O honored friend!
May Christ's calm spirit o'er thee bend!
May shining angels hover near!
May angel-voices whisper cheer!
And may a shining angel-band
Bear thy soul to that "better land," —
That "better land," we know not where,
Yet hope and pray to meet thee there!
And, waiting, hoping, gaze afar,
And pray to find those gates ajar.
" *Rex tremendæ majestatis,*
Qui salvandos salvas gratis,
Salva te! fons pietatis: "
Salva te! Rex majestatis.

WHEN THE POET DIES.

"And the Poet, faithful and far-seeing,
  Sees, alike in stars and flowers, a part
Of the self-same, universal being
  Which is throbbing in his brain and heart."
                                    LONGFELLOW.

I.

'Tis said, that, when the Poet dies,
  Great Nature mourns her gifted child,
And Nature's various voices rise
  In solemn requiem, sweet and wild;
And that the Poet's loved abodes,
  His sylvan haunts by wood and stream,
Are vocal with wild spirit-odes,
  Like the weird music of a dream.

II.

That dark, sad pines on hill-tops lone,
  And murmuring brooks in valleys deep,
For the dead Minstrel sigh and moan,
  And murmur dirges round his sleep:

The low, soft winds, in mournful sighs,
    Breathe out their sorrows o'er his head;
And sorrowing tears, from cold, gray skies,
    Drop down upon his lowly bed.

III.

The brave old trees that stretched their arms
    To shield him with their grateful shade, —
Ah! who shall celebrate their charms
    When their loved Bard is lowly laid?
When their green leaves — all sear and brown,
    And whirling in the " dance of death " —
To the cold earth go sailing down,
    Scattered by autumn's chilling breath, —

IV.

Oh! who shall celebrate their fall,
    And sing their beauty, as they fade,
When he — so loved, and loving all —
    In the dark, silent tomb is laid?
'Tis meet that flowers distill their tears,
    And breathe sweet perfumes round the tomb
Of the loved Bard, who, through long years,
    Has sung their beauty and their bloom.

V.

'Tis meet the wondrous-flaming stars
    Shed their kind influence round his name ;
For he, with all a Poet's cares,
    Has sung of their mysterious flame.
O child of Nature ! son of song !
    High priest in Nature's holy fane !
'Tis meet that Nature's voices strong
    Should echo back the Poet's name.

VI.

Let distant thunder's dying groan
    Mourn Nature's gifted child of song !
Let lightnings blaze from zone to zone,
    To light his fleeting shade along !
And let great Nature's voices raise
    One mighty anthem — deep and long —
To celebrate, with Nature's praise,
    Her dying Bard ! her son of song !